Dinosorcerers

NATHAN MILNER

DEDICATION

To my parents

CHAPTER ONE

Charlie gripped his parents' hands in his and dragged them onward like two dour kites.

His sneakers squeaked across the museum's tile floor and behind him his parents mumbled about taking it all in and enjoying the day.

"Stop running," his sister Emily hissed. "Everyone is looking at us."

Charlie barely heard her. He was following a series of signs that read "Dinosaur Exhibit, Hall C;" "Dinosaur Exhibit, Turn Right;" then "Turn Back, You Missed the Dinosaurs" (Charlie had to use the restroom); and finally, "Dinosaurs, Straight Ahead."

Charlie saw looming before him a huge banner that read "Dinosaurs Alive." The letters in "Alive" had been formed out of bones. They looked more like human tibia and humerus than the bones of any known dinosaur but Charlie appreciated the effort, nonetheless.

Below the banner, a large crowd milled in front of the exhibit and Charlie vowed never to forgive his sister for having taken so long to get ready. Now they would have to wait in line.

Charlie let go of his parents and dove into the crowd. He ducked. He swerved. He slipped through any gap he found between two people, whether he fit or not.

When Charlie reached the front of the crowd, he expected to see vast hall filled with lifelike representations of sauropods, theropods and pteranodons. Instead, Charlie discovered a plain white curtain.

A tall man dressed in paint-stained overalls, probably the curator of the museum, emerged from behind the curtain and the crowd began to cheer.

He must be here to open the red velvet rope holding them back and invite them all into the exhibit.

The man didn't speak but he held up one finger indicating they would have to wait one more...something. One minute? One second? One year?

Charlie was mentally searching for a loophole in rule #3 of the 18 rules his parents had read him before they'd gotten into the car that morning: no shouting.

Could he make a case that yelling was not the same as shouting?

The man turned his back to the crowd; yanked on the curtain, struggling to pull it open; and then ducked underneath it. He left behind a piece of paper taped with thick blue painters' tape to the sheet.

Why was the museum's curator carrying painters' tape? Something was written on the paper but it was just a little too far away for Charlie to read.

Charlie heard groans and the crowd began to disperse. "What does it say, guys? What does it say?" Charlie asked strangers as they passed.

He fought through a wave of people moving in the opposite direction toward the front of the line. When he finally stood close enough to make out the words written on the paper in thick black marker, he read the sign aloud: "Dinosaur exhibit closed for renovations."

And that was when Charlie just flat-out broke rule #3.

Charlie's family followed the shouts to find him. "Oh, no," his mom said, reading the sign for herself. "Well, look at it this way - now we get to spend more time at the 'Minerals of Northern Ohio' exhibit." Charlie was trying desperately not to look at it that way.

"Buck up, bud," said Charlie's father. "You've already waited 65 million years for those fossils. What's one more year going to hurt? We'll be back for your tenth birthday."

His sister approached. It was her turn to say something that didn't really help at all. She opened her mouth to speak but then Charlie shot her a look, one that siblings share sometimes, that said, "Stop! I have reached the limits of my restraint and whatever you have to add – reassurance, mockery or distraction – will only send me into a tantrum the likes of which has not been seen since the Stolen Blanket Incident of last weekend. The scene I would make would be epic and terminally embarrassing to anyone within a 15-foot radius."

Emily listened to what the look had to say and closed her mouth firmly.

"We should go," Emily said taking her father's hand and leading him away.

"I know you're disappointed, honey," Charlie's mom said. "But there are lots of other exhibits here at the museum. We're going to have a fun day so let's try to forget about dinosaurs for a little while, ok? We'll be at the 'History of

7

Cardboard' exhibit when you're ready." His mother walked away.

Forget about dinosaurs? That was absurd.

Forget that a type of triceratops called maximum triceratops could blow its nose so low and strong that it shook the ground like an earthquake? Not likely.

Should he forget that the dinosaur with the longest name was the micropachycephalosaurus? No, never.

Charlie stood in front of the closed dinosaur exhibit and, as he did in times of stress, he asked himself, "What would a velociraptor do?" Considered the smartest of the dinosaurs based on the size of its brain, thinking like a velociraptor helped Charlie make wise choices.

He looked at the velvet rope...not really much of a barrier to a predator who had to contend with ankylosaurus armor or the deadly horn of a styracosaurus. And that curtain...why, the man in the Speedy Painting coveralls had slipped right through it and he was a museum curator, not a velociraptor.

The answer was clear. Charlie scanned the room quickly to see if anyone was watching then he ducked under the rope, dashed through the sheet and tripped over his shoelace.

Just like a velociraptor would.

CHAPTER TWO

Charlie landed on the tile floor of the museum's dinosaur exhibit with a thud that echoed through the open room.

He scrambled to his feet and leapt behind a pedestal that held a replica of a maiasaura nest, seeking cover. His back hit the column so hard that he heard the eggs rattle against each other above him.

He listened, waiting for another sound, an adult's voice. "Hey, you there. What are you doing in here? Can't you read the sign? You need to leave this area, and as punishment, we won't kick you out of the rest of the museum," is how it might have sounded. But instead, Charlie heard only the sound of the eggs rocking softly back into place.

Charlie peeked out from behind the pedestal and the room appeared to be empty.

Empty except for more dinosaurs than he had ever dreamt of. Full skeletons, life-size models, animatronic robots that spoke in anachronistic Southern dialects.

He couldn't decide where to start.

Well, of course, he would start at the beginning: the

Triassic Period. Charlie made his way to the Triassic dinosaurs. Some of the earliest and smallest dinosaurs, these guys weren't ready yet to rule the world but, in Charlie's estimation, there were still some hall of fame dinos from this period.

A model coelophysis head you could wear like a helmet allowed Charlie to sample the stereoscopic vision that made these carnivores such dangerous predators.

Charlie spotted a pack of tiny two-legged dinosaurs with thin curled hands and he knew he had found the eoraptors, possibly the earliest reptile to be classified as a dinosaur. If they had lived at the time of the sauropods, they would have looked like ants next to those giants. They were only about half as tall as Charlie himself.

Charlie squatted down, tucked his arms back and imagined himself running with a pack of eoraptors through a Triassic marsh. We're a gang, Charlie thought. We watch each other's backs, protect our own.

After spending some time with the coelophysis and eoraptors, Charlie was ready to move on to the Jurassic, the period when dinosaurs grew to the size of skyscrapers. During this time dinosaurs ruled over not only the earth, flying reptiles like archeopteryx and rhamphorhynchus soared the skies and ichthyosaurs swam the seas.

He found a stegosaurus, his favorite Jurassic dinosaur. He got down on all fours and imagined himself grazing on ferns, soaking up the sun through the plates on his back which acted like big built-in solar panels and lazily swinging his spike-studded tail to warn away any potential predators. It was a simple, carefree life.

Charlie checked out the allosaurus and brachiosaurus before moving past the Jurassic section.

He had been in the dinosaur exhibit for close to an hour now. His parents would be missing him soon but there was no way he could leave without having explored everything.

Just the Cretaceous Period remained but it featured many of the coolest and best dinosaurs. This could take a while.

Charlie ran to the T Rex. He stood next to it. His head only reached as high as its ankle. Its mouth hung open. Charlie gazed up and imagined the mighty T Rex splitting the silence of the hall with a deafening roar. He could practically hear it. But what he heard instead was infinitely more terrifying – footsteps.

He wasn't alone in the hall.

Charlie dashed to the nearby scene which displayed baby triceratops hatching from enormous eggs. He dove into an empty egg and pulled the matching fragment of shell on top of himself. He tilted it open just enough to peek out.

Charlie saw a man walking through the hall and muttering to himself.

The man looked tall, taller than Charlie's father, but he was stooped and stiff, more like Charlie's grandfather. He wore a long poncho and a wide-brimmed floppy hat.

The man shuffled from one scene to another jotting down notes on loose scraps of paper he drew from within his poncho.

Charlie guessed he must be some kind of inspector verifying the accuracy of the museum's dinosaur information. About time too, Charlie thought.

Just last month his parents had taken him to a science exhibition near their home where Charlie discovered a diorama featuring a caveman riding a pteranodon. Charlie rushed the stage, wrestled the microphone from one of the presenters and began to list the numerous factual inaccuracies he had spotted in their scientific displays before he was led away.

And that is why Charlie is no longer welcome at the Northford Elementary School science fair.

The man had examined every other nearby exhibit and began making his way toward the eggs. Charlie lowered the shell hoping that from the outside it would appear sealed.

Charlie held his breath as he heard the man poking around the eggs, talking to himself and...sniffing?

Charlie's egg was lifted and shaken forcefully the same way that Charlie shook all of his Christmas presents before opening them. Charlie gripped the shell top with all of his strength to keep it from flying off.

Suddenly, Charlie heard more voices, several of them, talking loudly and laughing.

His egg dropped to the ground and the shock jolted the shell top loose, just enough to allow Charlie to see the man in the poncho looking frantically around the room.

From the far end of the room, men in overalls had entered through an outside door.

"Oh, bother," the man in the poncho grumbled. He spun away from Charlie's egg and dashed out of sight. As he did, something hit the side of Charlie's egg and sent it rolling across the tile.

Charlie heard the man yelp something like "ow, my pail," but it might have been "snail" or "tail." He didn't have time to consider which made the most sense because he was rolling.

Charlie dove from the egg just before it collided with an allosaurus shin and exploded into pieces. He had escaped the egg but now Charlie lay on the floor out in the open as the overalled men walked closer.

He had only seconds before they spotted him.

Charlie looked around and saw a door. It was his only hope. He ran to the door, tossed it open and threw himself inside.

It was dark and cramped inside. No matter which direction he turned, Charlie encountered something heavy and pebbled. Charlie felt like he was being buried under a pile of basketballs. He felt like he was trapped in the cushions of a leather sofa.

"If you wouldn't mind," a voice said softly, "would you please stop stepping on my tail?"

Tail. It was "tail" he said.

CHAPTER THREE

Charlie listened from the dark closet as the voices outside grew louder, closer.

"...so I said, 'Get your own ambulance, buddy.' You shoulda seen the look on his face - hey...which one of you guys broke the egg?" A heavy, seasoned voice asked.

"It wasn't me, boss. I was on my lunch break." Said the squeaky, squirrelly voice.

"Wasn't me," added the tall, sandy-haired voice. "I took a walk around the block. I wanted to get some eggs-ercise."

"Very funny, Tommy. This is not the time for jokes. The museum lady was very clear – we're not supposed to touch any of the displays, just the walls."

"What are we going to do, boss?"

"He's right. We need to *hatch* a plan."

"I know what you're doing, Tommy, and I am not in the mood."

"Boss, my cousin can fix anything. Let's pick up the pieces, take them over to his garage and then we'll bring it back here, good as new."

"Good as old. It's a fossil, you know."

"Tommy, I'm losing my patience with you. Phil, your cousin fixes cars. What does he know about dinosaurs?"

"Trust me. He can fix anything."

"Ok, we gotta do something," the boss said. "Sweep those pieces into a box and let's go see your cousin."

Their footsteps faded and the door slammed. When Charlie felt that it was safe to speak he let loose with all the questions he'd been holding in. "What were you doing out there?" Charlie asked the man in the closet with him. "Why are you hiding? You don't belong in here, do you? Did you say you have a tail?"

"I could ask you many of the same questions, could I not," came the low, rumbling reply. "Except the one about the tail."

Charlie twisted the knob of the closet door. The door burst open and they both spilled out onto the floor. The man's hat slipped off and Charlie saw deep creases lining his face. The man's skin looked a greenish shade of grey. He looked like he was in no condition to be tumbling out of closets.

"Are you okay, mister?" Charlie asked.

"Yes, yes. I've been through worse." The stranger got to his knees with some effort and replaced his hat snugly atop his head. He still looked slightly dazed. "If you wouldn't mind helping me collect my things, though." During their forceful ejection from the closet, the man's papers had flown out of his poncho in every direction. They now lay scattered all over the floor.

"Yeah, sure." Charlie bent and began to gather up the loose pages. "So are you an inspector or researcher or something? What were you writing anyway?"

"What was I writing?" The man asked with some confusion. "When?"

Charlie couldn't resist taking a peek at the papers in his arms. They were covered in crude drawings of dinosaurs with arrows pointing to key features and notes on the dinosaur's diet or size copied from the museum's informational plaques. A drawing of a carnotaurus had "Sharp!! Look out!" scribbled near its teeth. In large, underlined letters above a drawing of a triceratops were the words: "THREE horns."

"No one asked you to touch those," the man groused nervously snatching the papers out of Charlie's arms. "And I'm sure no one told you to read them."

"You asked me to help pick them up, remember? It was 30 seconds ago." Charlie was growing more and more worried about the fall the man had taken. Charlie handed him back the pages and the man tucked them hastily inside his robes.

"Oh, I did? Thank you."

"Seems like you're brushing up on the basics," Charlie said. "Are you just learning about dinosaurs?"

"'Learning' is not quite right. I would say...remembering."

They stood in awkward silence for a moment, both of them unsure if their interaction was complete. Finally, Charlie spoke up: "So...can I ask about the tail?"

"No."

"Right. I had to ask, you know."

"Right." More awkward silence.

"Anyway, I should get back to my family," Charlie said. He started to walk away then turned back. "Oh, and the allosaurus wasn't really 20 feet tall. In your notes, I happened to see that. The display is actually inaccurate. It would have been closer to 40 feet."

"Thank you, again," the man said. "That's twice you've helped me today." He leaned in very close and Charlie saw his face a little more clearly under the hat. It was long and flat with wide-set nostrils that flared when he breathed. His eyes were bright and clear. "You know a great deal about dinosaurs, don't you?"

"Yeah, I guess I do." The man's face was still uncomfortably close and his breathing blew back Charlie's hair.

"My name is Beeon," the man held out a shaky, wrinkled hand to Charlie.

"Charlie," Charlie replied, shaking his hand. "Nice to meet you."

Charlie was ready to return to his family. Sneaking into the exhibit had been fun but then the stranger had gone and made it weird.

He had no idea how weird it would get.

CHAPTER FOUR

"Charlie, where have you been?" his mother asked him. "Your father was talking to you for ten minutes before he realized it was a trash can."

"I broke into the dinosaur exhibit, hid inside an egg and met a mysterious, tailed man," Charlie replied.

"Stop fooling around, Charlie."

Charlie rejoined his family and the rest of the museum passed in a kind of blur.

Not the good kind of blur when you're having fun and time is flying by, like when dad holds your hands and spins you around in a circle and your feet lift off the ground and your shoes feel like they might fly off.

It was more the kind of blur that happens when you focus very hard on something – like a bird on a branch or a picture in a book – and everything outside of where you're focusing becomes dull and grey.

Charlie could only think about what had happened in the dinosaur exhibit, of the man he had met and his strange notes. Every possible explanation Charlie could imagine for who the man was and what he was doing was more interesting than the real world around him.

From his family's voices to an interactive simulation of the lifespan of shrimp, very little penetrated this haze in which Charlie found himself surrounded. That is, until a commotion near the entrance hall caught Charlie's attention.

He heard raised voices then shouts and angry murmurs from the crowd waiting to enter the museum as they broke apart to allow someone through. Emerging from the crowd, Charlie saw the man he had met in the dinosaur exhibit being escorted by a security guard.

The guard shoved him forward while Beeon seemed to be trying to explain himself.

They arrived at a desk where a taller guard with more pins on his hat sat waiting. Charlie stepped close enough to hear what they were saying.

"...found this guy snooping around the dino exhibit. I think he might be a spy from the Wentworth Museum out in Forksburg," the guard said.

"That's not true," Beeon protested. "I wasn't spying. I – I lost something in there. Yes, something important that I needed to find."

"Oh, yeah? What?" The guard asked.

"Uh...my...." Beeon's eyes scanned the museum frantically. He settled on a boy walked by eating from a bag of candy. "My lollipop!"

He was going down in flames. Charlie couldn't just sit back and watch.

"Hey, Tony," Charlie shouted as he approached the guards and Beeon turned to stare at him. Charlie directed his words at Beeon as he spoke but Beeon showed no reaction. "Yeah, Tony. I'm talking to you. Why aren't you back at work?"

"I...well," Beeon stuttered.

"Just save it; I don't want to hear any excuses. Did you get what we needed?"

"Wait, who are you?" The guard who'd captured Beeon asked rather aggressively.

"We're part of Paulie's crew," Charlie said.

"Paulie's crew? You're eight."

"Nine. Today is my birthday; thank you very much. I just supervise. Guys like Tony here do the heavy lifting."

"Where is Paulie anyway?" The standing guard asked.

"Well, we were doing our job in dinosaur exhibit, which is...uh, what's the term for that?"

"Painting the walls?" The sitting guard offered.

"Right. Painting the walls. And there was an issue with the paint thing...you know…"

"The sprayer?"

"Yes. The sprayer broke. Just a complete failure of the...whatchamacallit…"

"The D6 Hoison Head Release Valve?"

"The D7 Hoison Head Release Valve. What kind of outfit do you think we're running?"

"Well, did you take it to Phil's cousin because - "

"He can fix anything," Charlie interrupted. "That's exactly what I said. And that's where they are now. Paulie told us to stay here and make sure the valve failure didn't damage any of the displays. That's what Tony here was doing before you started pushing him around."

The sitting guard gave the other guard the kind of look Charlie's dad gave him when he was "not mad, just disappointed."

"I'm very sorry for the way Hastings treated you," the

sitting guard said. "He's new here and he still has a lot to learn. You gentlemen are free to go."

Charlie was a little amazed that had worked. He took Beeon's hand and began to lead him, stepping quickly, but not running, to get away from the guards before they changed their minds.

"Wait just one minute," the sitting guard shouted and Charlie and Beeon froze in their tracks.

Charlie turned back cautiously. "Yes?"

"Hastings has something to tell you."

The guard, Hastings, shuffled forward with his hands clasped before him and his eyes turned to the ground. In a soft voice he said, "happy birthday."

CHAPTER FIVE

As soon as they were out of the guards' sight, Charlie and Beeon sprinted toward the museum entrance. Only when they had made it outside, at the top of the front steps, did they feel safely outside the jurisdictional reach of the museum guards.

Beeon turned to Charlie then. "That is *two* times you've helped me today, young man. Thank you."

"Three times, actually," Charlie corrected. "I helped pick up your notes. Then I told you about an error in one of the notes. So this is three."

"Three?!" Beeon leaned down again to look Charlie right in the eyes. "You have now helped me three times. Among my kind, when someone helps you three times, you owe them a life debt."

"Um, ok, what does that mean," Charlie asked.

"Ask of me anything you would like and I must comply," Beeon said. "Choose carefully."

Charlie didn't have to think hard about what he wanted from Beeon. He'd been thinking about it ever since he met him. "I guess I'd just like to know who you are and what you were doing in the museum."

Beeon sighed. "Well, that is complicated. It's difficult to describe…. You don't want ice cream? Most kids want ice cream and I believe there is a shop around the corner."

"No. I'd prefer answers."

"CHARLIE!" Charlie's mother's voice rang out from inside the museum. His family must have noticed him missing.

"Charlie!" Now it was his father's voice Charlie heard, followed shortly after by a less enthusiastic "charlie." His sister was doing her part but no one could make her like it.

"It will take some time to explain," Beeon said. "Meet me at the caves next to the park off Cottonwood Lane tomorrow afternoon."

"I can come after school," Charlie said.

"Good."

Charlie's father emerged from the museum entrance just as Beeon had turned to walk down the steps. "He's out here, guys. Charlie, what are you doing out here? We were looking everywhere for you."

"Sorry, dad. Just a little too much excitement, I guess. I had to come out here to catch my breath."

"I think we all had enough museum excitement for one day," Charlie's dad said. "Are you ready to go?"

"Yes, thank you," Charlie replied, his voice distant and his eyes staring somewhere far away.

Charlie didn't know how he would survive the wait until tomorrow afternoon. He decided, for his own sanity, to enter a sort of walking, talking hibernation. He set his "away" message to: "Yes, thank you." His reasoning seemed simple enough. It was always better to say "yes" than "no," and the "thank you" at the end helped smooth over any potential problems.

"Wow. What a polite kid," Charlie's dad said. "I think a kid like that deserves ice cream. Does that sound good?"

"Yes, thank you."

The away message worked remarkably well. It only got him into trouble once over the next 24 hours. His sister caught on around dinnertime and asked, "Hey, Charlie, would you like to wash and dry the dishes all by yourself tonight?" Otherwise, it worked perfectly.

***

Charlie arrived home from school after successfully hibernating since the previous afternoon, slung his backpack over a corner of a chair in the kitchen and shouted to his mother that he was going to the park.

At the far corner of the park, beyond the jungle gym and the open field of grass where Charlie played soccer in the fall, there was a series of caves.

Some of the caves were only a few feet deep; some were deep enough to swallow a soccer ball and never give it back. But one of them – the one marked with a small, tin sign that read, "Danger! Stay Out!!" – stretched on for miles, according to what Charlie had heard from a couple members of his soccer team.

Charlie had heard that either a bear or a witch or a ghost of a goalie lived in the cave and that the cave reached to the core of the Earth where the witch traveled to brew her most powerful potions. Charlie honestly felt as excited to find out which of these rumors was true as he was to learn Beeon's story.

Charlie walked out to where the grass turned to bare, hard-packed dirt and then to the start of a loose, rocky wilderness. He stood at the sign in front of the cave and waited. Minutes passed.

This is where Beeon had told him to meet; he was sure of it.

As time stretched on like a rubber band aimed at him by his sister, Charlie watched kids on the swings and thought maybe he could wait from there. But then he might miss Beeon if he didn't stand in this exact spot where the trees parted and allowed a clear view from one end of the park to the other.

While he was thinking all of this, Charlie heard humming.

He whirled around. There was no one within 100 yards of him. He followed the sound where it was loudest and Charlie realized it was coming from inside the cave.

Charlie stood at the mouth of the cave and listened. The humming resounded from within and he heard something like glasses clinking against each other. Beeon couldn't have meant inside the cave, could he?

Charlie walked in a few steps and from around the corner ahead, he began to see a faint flickering light. As he rounded the corner, Charlie shouted, "Beeon, is that you?"

The light went out.

Charlie had followed the light too deep into the cave, too far from the entrance. He was surrounded by pure darkness now and he was terrified. The humming had stopped too – all sound, in fact. It was silent and dark.

He groped for the sides of the cave. "Beeon! Beeon, please. It's me, Charlie." And as a chorus of "Charlie"s bounced off the walls and echoed around him, he heard one more low voice in the darkness say, "Charlie who?"

"Charlie from the museum, remember? I helped you *three* times." He emphasized the number the same way that Beeon had.

In a flash, the passage around him filled with light. The sudden illumination left Charlie more blind than he had been in the dark.

"Charlie, hmm?"

Charlie, squinting and blinking, still couldn't locate the source of the voice but he continued walking forward. As his eyes adjusted to the light, Charlie found himself in a large open chamber with candles burning every few feet along the rough rock walls.

Translucent white crystals hung from the ceiling, catching and reflecting the candles' light. And there, across the room, Charlie saw Beeon standing behind a simple wooden table with a collection of jars and vials in front of him.

Beeon barely looked up from his work to address Charlie. "Three times, you say? And what did you ask for?"

"I wanted to know what you were doing at the museum yesterday," Charlie said.

"Ah, well, it's good timing then," Beeon said. "Instead of telling you that story, I can show you."

CHAPTER SIX

"Here, drink this."

Beeon pushed a vial toward Charlie. Charlie considered it for only a moment then began to lift the vial to his lips.

"No, wait!" Beeon snatched the vial before the first drop spilled out.

He grabbed a wad of purple leaves and squeezed them over the vial until three drops of dark fluid fell into the liquid in the vial causing it to bubble lightly.

"Almost forgot gandydill," Beeon chuckled. "Wouldn't have worked without that...and it would have paralyzed you for two or three years. All set now."

Charlie took the vial and lifted it very slowly to give Beeon plenty of time to search his memory for additional ingredients but Beeon just sat watching expectantly. Charlie drank.

The potion in the vial tasted like puddle water after a family of worms had all taken their baths in it. Charlie set the vial down and waited for something to happen.

"Should I feel something?"

"The effects can be unpredictable," Beeon said. "It might take five minutes. It might hit you tomorrow morning at 10 o'clock."

"Tomorrow morning?! I have to go to school," Charlie shouted. He pounded the table but instead of the emphatic thump he was hoping for, it sounded soft and wet. The table felt like Jello under his fist.

"Most of my class already thinks I'm weird."

Beeon turned away and shuffled through some notes. He wasn't walking away but he was shrinking.

"And then this potion," Charlie continued, "whatever it does – is going to turn me into a newt or something in the middle of class?"

The candles along the walls began to slide toward each other as the walls themselves melted away. The candles finally met and merged growing brighter and redder. The ball of light rose slightly then plopped down on the now-visible horizon, forming a low, early evening sun.

Charlie looked around him. The cave walls were gone now. He stood on a vast, open plain covered in thick, ankle-tall grass.

He turned slowly and there behind him were a series of rock ledges rising up in steps. And sitting or standing on those ledges, as their anatomies allowed, were dinosaurs, five rows high.

There must have been close to 30 of them – triceratops next to T Rex, archeopteryx hovering around the head of an apatosaurus. And there, in the front row, sat the shrunken Beeon.

Charlie's image of Beeon had been shifting since he'd first met him – an old man, an old man with a tail, something other than a man. But seeing him smoothed out and young,

28

Charlie realized for the first time what he was seeing when he looked at Beeon, an iguanodon. He was a dinosaur. They were all dinosaurs.

The young Beeon didn't talk to anyone. He fidgeted in his seat. It wasn't just that he was sitting next to huge brachiosaurs and giganotosaurs; even compared to the other iguanodons, Beeon looked small.

"Are these living dinosaurs?" Charlie asked.

"Living? No, just a memory. And a fading one at that," Beeon answered. "And not just dinosaurs. Dinosorcerers."

None of the dinosaurs around him reacted to Beeon speaking. It was as if he and Charlie were alone and not surrounded by walking, talking dinosaurs.

Charlie was scanning and identifying the rows of dinosaurs when he noticed suddenly that night seemed to have fallen around him. He was engulfed by a shadow the size of a swimming pool. Charlie looked up and saw a lambeosaurus who must have materialized out of thin air towering over him. The dinosaurs all fell silent.

"That is Quintus, our teacher. The first dinosorcerer," Beeon said.

Quintus paced back and forth before his students, thinking deeply. Then he began to speak or his mouth began to move but no sound came out. It was like watching a television set to mute.

He flailed his arms and gestured to the sky clearly very excited about something. The students' faces registered shock and dismay.

"He was very wise," Beeon said. "He studied the sky and he knew. He tried to warn the others. He told us...well, just listen to what he told us."

Slowly Quintus' voice became audible as if Beeon had

turned a volume knob. "...will destroy everything. Countless dinosaurs will be killed in the impact and after the impact, dirt and debris will cloud the air blocking out the sun. Plants will die. There will be no food."

"Can you stop it, sir?" A pteranodon near the back asked.

"No. Even I do not possess that kind of power."

"Did you tell the governors?" asked a smallish ankylosaurus.

"I told them, Taba. They don't believe me. They don't believe in anything we do here. I'm sorry to scare you, young ones, but you needed to know. And I'm sorry to burden you with this but I will need your help."

"We haven't finished our training," shouted a voice in the crowd.

"No, but you have achieved a great deal. Even our newest students – Beeon and Occidor," he gestured to Beeon in the front row and a corythosaurus sitting next to him, "have shown great promise and will be an asset in what we must do next. Now –" Quintus froze in the middle of his speech. The archaeopteryx hovering around her apatosaurus friend hung suspended in midair. The scene had been paused.

"That was the important part," Beeon said. "You'll see the plan shortly." He stood up from his seat and, for the first time, he looked behind himself. "That's strange...the last time I was here the stadium was nearly empty but...there's Monmo. Did you do this?"

"Do what?" Charlie asked.

Beeon's young face re-wrinkled with curiosity. "What do you believe happened next?" he asked Charlie.

"Well, the oviraptor in the third row - her name means 'egg thief' but it is well known that oviraptors are in fact strong protective mothers, guardians of eggs. She's been distracted ever since Quintus mentioned the meteor. She wants to get back to her nest to hold her eggs close."

From over his shoulder, Charlie heard the voice of Quintus resume right where it had left off. The archeopteryx started spinning again. The oviraptor fidgeted in her seat, glancing nervously to each side, tapping her foot. Then she stood suddenly, exited her row, excusing herself as she stepped on feet and tails. And when she reached the bottom of the stadium stairs, she sprinted off into the distance.

The scene froze again and Charlie realized Beeon was staring at him.

"Amazing."

CHAPTER SEVEN

"My memory has faded some," Beeon said. "I've forgotten many of the details. But you – you've filled them in...and more."

"I read a lot of books about dinosaurs," Charlie offered by way of explanation.

"I'm sure you do. It's more than that, though."

Beeon was staring at Charlie now, making him more than a little uncomfortable, when the world under their feet jerked forward suddenly and forcefully.

Charlie and Beeon hadn't moved but everything around them spun like a kaleidoscope. Charlie felt dizzy and sick.

The outdoor classroom was replaced by a cave very like the one Charlie had discovered Beeon in. Charlie wondered for a moment if they had left Beeon's memory and returned to the present.

As he shook his disorientation and took a closer look around him, however, Charlie noticed a key difference: in this cave, the books and potions were all carefully and neatly arranged. It was immaculate. In Beeon's cave, every surface –

tables, shelves, even the floor – was strewn with millions of years' worth of magical clutter.

As Charlie continued scanning the room, he discovered Quintus standing behind a roughhewn stone table near the back of the cave. Quintus, who stood as tall as Charlie's second-floor bedroom window, delicately arranged and rearranged items on the table as he waited for his students to take their seats.

A small group of his dinosaurs sat before him on the cave floor. Again Beeon and the wiry corythosaurus sat at the front. The group of students was clearly smaller than it had been in the outdoor classroom. Charlie wasn't sure if the others couldn't fit in the cave or if they'd been scared off by Quintus's predictions.

Quintus looked calmer than he had in the previous memory. The alarm he must have felt upon learning of the meteor hurtling toward Earth seemed to have given way to a fierce determination.

"Now watch, young ones," Quintus addressed his students, "this is very advanced magic." His small fingers were surprisingly graceful. They moved through the air as if they were tracing out eight different symbols simultaneously.

Quintus glanced down from time to time at the book open on the table in front of him. His hands twisted at the air like he was turning two invisible door knobs at the same time but the air resisted. His hands trembled and would not turn. Quintus refocused, gritting his wide, flat teeth. One hand went back to work tracing symbols in the air while the other wiped his brow and made quick notes in the book before him.

Once the other hand returned to effort of making magic, a blue mist began to take shape around his hands. At first

33

barely visible, the mist grew more solid as he worked. From a shapeless cloud sharp angles formed until a solid, sky-blue rectangle the size of the box Charlie's sneakers had come in hung in the air in front of Quintus.

He repeated the twisting motion. This time he encountered no resistance and the blue fell away to reveal a golden light. The students, even Charlie, felt a sudden draft in the cave.

"Dezzduan, please pick up the apple sitting on my desk." Quintus managed to speak calmly but he was straining to maintain the solidity of the box. Its edges rippled when he diverted his attention, threatening to collapse. The student Quintus had summoned approached the table and picked up the apple.

"Please throw the apple at the box," Quintus instructed.

"At you?" the student asked.

"At the box which is in front of me. If we both do our parts, I won't be hit."

The student drew his arm back and hurled the apple toward the box. As it left his hand, the apple curved wickedly upward, sailing right over the box and striking Quintus directly in the center of the forehead.

Quintus emitted an involuntary honk from his head crest. Occidor laughed a little too loud then collected himself and ran to fetch the apple from where it had landed.

The portal wobbled as Quintus struggled to regain his focus but after a moment he was holding it steady again.

"Can I try this time?" Occidor chirped while Dezzduan sat solemnly back on the cave floor.

"Yes, Occidor. But please be careful."

Occidor tossed the apple toward Quintus. It soared into the golden glow at the center of the box and slowly receded from view.

Quintus clapped his hands together and the box disappeared. He leaned forward, head down, elbows resting on the table and panted heavily as his students watched in silence.

"Now the tricky part," Quintus said.

He straightened himself and his hands began to move again. He seemed surer of himself this time, faster. He seldom consulted the book and within a minute or so, the blue mist appeared, solidified and opened onto the golden light.

This time, Quintus very slowly grasped the edges of the box and twisted them downward until the flat box lay parallel to the tabletop but hung three or four feet above it.

Once he had maneuvered it into position, Quintus gave the box one quick shake and the apple, the same apple Occidor had thrown, tumbled down onto the stone table.

Quintus squashed the box between his hands again.

"So," he said, "that is my plan. Any questions?"

Several students raised their hands.

"Yes," one of the students spoke up. "How will you make the portal big enough to fit the meteor? Just a small one looked very difficult."

"Oh, no," Quintus said. "The apple demonstration wasn't – the apple isn't the meteor, I'm afraid. The apple is you."

CHAPTER EIGHT

Quintus had turned his attention back to his book, busily scribbling notes when Beeon paused the scene, a look of anxious relief frozen on Quintus' face.

Charlie couldn't help feeling there was something strange about the corythosaurus. While the other dinosaurs wore blank or awkwardly paused expressions on their frozen faces, Occidor's eyes seemed to follow Charlie and Beeon wherever they moved about the memory.

He looked as if he might stand and join them at any moment.

"So what happened next?" Charlie asked.

"I'm not sure I remem-," Beeon started then stopped himself. He narrowed his eyes at Charlie. "Why don't you tell me?"

Charlie took a moment and surveyed the scene around him. The shelves of books neatly arranged; a cave floor with barely a trace of dirt; Quintus, an herbivore who needed to be on constant alert to avoid predators.

"He was careful," Charlie said. "And he was unsure of his

plan. I mean, who can blame him. Would he be able to make it big enough for an Apatosaurus to fit through and how long could he hold it open?"

"Therefore…" Beeon coaxed.

"He had a back-up plan, of course."

"Yes, I believe he did," Beeon said with some astonishment in his voice.

Beeon measured Charlie up across the still air of the cave still frozen in time. Charlie found it a little strange talking to young Beeon. Though still a foot or two taller than him, this Beeon felt to Charlie more like a peer, another kid he might have met in the halls at school or on the soccer field.

"I think you might be the element I was missing. The spell might actually work now," Beeon said, giddy with excitement.

"We need to get back to the present." Beeon pulled a vial from his pocket. "Drink this."

"No, wait," Charlie said, gently pushing back against the vial. "I want to see the rest."

"It's just what you've seen in science books," Beeon said pushing the vial more forcefully.

"I don't remember reading about talking dinosaurs who cast magic spells," Charlie grunted. "Unless I was absent that day."

They were now engaged in a reverse tug of war where they both pushed the vial in opposite directions.

Charlie gave one last serious shove against the vial and the world around them lurched forward. The cave spun away from them and Charlie and Beeon were suddenly standing in a field amid a strand of apple trees.

Beeon looked alarmed. "How did you do that?"

"I don't know," Charlie said. "I concentrated and I

pushed. Is this…did I…move us?"

Charlie looked around. Grasses swayed softly under a sky so blue, so clear that it must have been difficult to imagine it could contain a threat to the dinosaurs' very existence.

The dinosorcerers were scattered about the field, gathered in small groups and practicing magic. Quintus walked among them, giving instruction or tips or encouragement as needed.

Charlie turned and noticed that Beeon was no longer standing by his side. Beeon had fallen into his memory role and followed closely behind Quintus wherever he walked. Beeon and Occidor, Quintus' two youngest students, had to follow and watch as the other students practiced their magic.

Quintus carried himself differently today. He looked joyful, Charlie thought. He had confidence in his plan. His students were giving him good reason to feel that way.

A group of older students took turns standing under an apple tree. Each student stepped forward, took their position beneath the branches of the tree and bowed their heads. They chanted softly and, slowly, a bubble began to form near their feet.

The bubble grew wider and taller, swallowing the dinosorcerer performing the spell until it had formed a cloudy dome over them. The way in which the dome inflated, gently and with obvious effort, reminded Charlie of blowing bubble gum bubbles with his sister in the backseat of the car on long drives.

When the bubble was ready, one of the other dinosaurs in the group shook the tree violently until apples rained down from the branches. The apples bounced harmlessly off of the domes and Quintus was pleased.

"It won't stop a meteorite," Quintus said, "but falling debris, yes."

Some bubbles were larger than others. Some formed a solid shield hiding the dinosaur inside from view; others were as light as mist. But they all stopped apples – and, on one occasion when an over enthusiastic T Rex shook a bit too zealously, even the tree itself.

Happy with what he saw from these students, Quintus walked on to the next group with Beeon and Occidor following him and Charlie following them.

The next group of students had divided themselves up into pairs. As they approached, a troodon was gazing intently into the eyes of his stegosaurus partner. The troodon murmured soft words just below Charlie's hearing. It had the effect of making Charlie want to lean in closer; the troodon's partner did just that.

Charlie started to creep closer when Beeon extended an arm and stopped him.

The stegosaurus visibly stiffened, eyes wide and glassy. The troodon broke eye contact with his partner and spoke out loud. "Alright, Montibec, if you look behind you, you'll notice that the spikes on your tail are now gone. No more sharp, deadly bone daggers at the end of your tail. No, instead you will find the ripest, juiciest, sweetest-smelling bunch of gingko berries you have ever encountered in your life."

The stegosaurus's tail hadn't changed at all but he was looking at it as if everything his partner said were true. He swung his tail madly toward his mouth forcing the other students to drop to the ground to avoid being spiked. His beak snapped at the air coming up several feet short of the illusory gingkos. He whipped his tail to the other side and tried again with no luck. The stegosaurus spun in a circle chasing his tail, turning faster and faster and more out of control until the dinosaur tornado he'd formed bowled over three other students and rolled down the hill.

"Wonderful, wonderful," Quintus clapped.

Quintus turned and spoke to the entire group practicing this spell. "Now I despise hypnotism. Our abilities should never be used to subvert another dinosaur's free will. But there are many who, even when they see the meteor with their own eyes, will refuse to believe in dinosorcery and will resist accompanying us. If we have exhausted all other methods of persuasion, we will have to resort to desperate measures to coax them into the portal."

Having made himself clear on the subject, Quintus added, "Please, carry on."

As they continued walking about the field, Charlie saw groups of dinosaurs practicing lifting heavy boulders, a skill that would prepare them to clear debris or build floodwalls. Still others worked on a spell that would allow them to extinguish small fires.

Charlie watched as a velociraptor easily raised a boulder over her head. To add to the degree of difficulty, she lifted a second and started them spinning in the air like she was juggling tennis balls.

The massive rocks moved swiftly and smoothly through the air. The velociraptor seemed in complete control until one of the boulders sailed off course. Quintus, Occidor and Beeon had no time to react as the boulder screamed toward them.

The rogue boulder landed just feet away from the master and his two young students before, with a sickening lurch, it rolled once more and came to rest on Quintus's tail.

The yelp had barely escaped his mouth before the velociraptor had regained control of the boulder and lifted it from her master's tail. "I'm so sorry, sir," she said. "I don't know what happened. It was like something was pulling on it suddenly."

"Be more careful, you fool!" Occidor screeched.

"Occidor!" Quintus cut him off. "It's fine. Nothing a little ice won't fix."

Beeon paused the scene. "It would seem you've seen enough now," Beeon said. "Let us return to my cave in the present."

"You didn't have a job?" Charlie asked.

"No. Too young, I'm afraid."

The explanation seemed odd. How could Quintus not make use of every available dinosorcerer in this dire time? Charlie thought he would like to see more and the scene resumed.

Quintus gave his encouragement to the last cluster of students Beeon and Occidor still trailing him.

"This is enough," Beeon said emphatically and tried to pause the memory again but he only managed to slow it to half speed.

As a result it was even harder for Charlie to miss the moment when Quintus turned, looked at his two youngest students and said in a slow-motion voice, "And now, last and most important, we come to my plans for you."

CHAPTER NINE

"Charlie, I don't want to do this," Beeon said.

Beeon turned to Charlie and his young face suddenly took on all of the gravity and seriousness of the older Beeon. In the dinosorcerer's eyes, Charlie saw a lifetime of experience and loss and he couldn't imagine forcing him to go on.

"Yes, you're right," Charlie said, pausing the scene. "We should get back to the cave."

The dinosaurs around them – frozen in the midst of inflating magical shields or levitating boulders – began to fade from view. They lost their central mass first leaving only a thin outline and then the outline was scratched out as if by eraser. It looked like a coloring book picture in reverse.

The bright blue sky above the apple trees darkened ominously, clouds sweeping in from over the horizon, swarming together and solidifying into the cave's crystal-studded ceiling.

Leaves and apples dropped from the trees in one loud flumpf. The tree trunks melted into tables, chairs and shelves and then Charlie and Beeon were back in the cave.

Beeon stood before Charlie in the flickering candle light looking older. Not just older than he'd been in the memory but older than when they'd left. He groaned wearily and retreated toward the back of the cave.

"Join me over here, Charlie, by the fire," Beeon called. A pair of high-backed chairs sat arranged in front of a rough fireplace set into the cave wall. "I can't remember them," Beeon said speaking more to the fire than Charlie.

"I go to museums and look at bones to try to bring it back – some small echo of their voices, just a shadow of their smiles. I revisit my memories hoping they'll become clearer with more information but they're fading."

"Millions of years I spent, working to create a spell that might bring them back and to master it. Now I've lost my memories just when I needed them most. But I believe you can help me there," Beeon continued, his weariness fading and excitement rising as he went on.

"You were wonderful today. Details I hadn't seen or remembered in millennia. Charlie, you know very much and you feel even more. With you performing the spell, I am sure that it will work."

Beeon looked expectantly at Charlie like he'd just offered Charlie a homemade chocolate chip cookie and was waiting to see how he would like it. To Charlie though, the cookie looked a little stale and like the cook might've mistakenly replaced the chocolate chips with pebbles.

"I'm not sure I understand. What will work?" Charlie asked. "I don't know any spells."

"No, no, of course you don't. Not yet. I'll teach you," Beeon said. "It's about time I had an apprentice. It's just the one spell. This spell, if it works, will allow me to communicate with the others, the ones who made it into the portal."

Charlie suddenly grasped the weight of what Beeon was saying. "The apples? The plan worked?"

"For some, yes. For all those poor fossils in your museums, no."

"But – but if the portal worked, why don't you make another? Just go where they went?"

"The spell is…complicated. A caster must know the exact location where the portal will open. And that is a piece of information that Quintus did not have an opportunity to pass on to me," Beeon grew quiet as he remembered his former teacher.

When the silence had grown uncomfortable, Charlie started to ease himself out of his chair. "You know it's been a long day. I'll come back another day and we can work on the spell."

"The spell?" Beeon muttered to himself. "The spell!" He jumped from his chair and retrieved his spell book from the shelf. Charlie recognized it almost immediately as Quintus's spell book.

Beeon threw the book open and pointed to a page. "With this spell we can talk to them. And they can tell me where they are. And then, Charlie, I can go there too."

Next to the spell Beeon was pointing at, Charlie noticed ragged edges where several pages had been torn from the book. And following the missing pages, several pages were marked with three long, thin tears as if claws had been dragged over them.

Something strange had happened on Departure Day; that much was clear to Charlie. But what it was and who was responsible remained frustratingly unclear. Although Beeon was unwilling to talk about it, Charlie now saw an opportunity to find the answers that Beeon refused to give. He felt the beginnings of a plan starting to take shape.

"You know what," Charlie said, trying not to sound overeager. "Let's do it."

CHAPTER TEN

Beeon wasted little time in making preparations for the spell casting. He swept clear a space on his stone table where he laid the open spell book. He ushered Charlie to a spot where the boy would have a view of both the book and Beeon's movements. And they were ready to begin.

"Ok. Follow my lead," Beeon said moving his hands slowly through the air just as Charlie had seen Quintus do.

Charlie imitated the motions as best he could. The hand movements came easily enough but Charlie had more fingers to contend with and his extra four digits seemed only to be getting in the way when he watched how nimbly Beeon's sculpted the air.

"Repeat the words you see in the book," Beeon said. The handwriting was tall and thin, hard to read, and the words were in some saurian language but Charlie did his best.

"Haasim, sosoctha, khashla...."

"Good. Now I want you to concentrate very hard on one of the dinosaurs you saw in my memory – the triceratops, perhaps. Picture him clearly in your mind. Make a connection. But don't stop there. Go beyond how he looks. What is he like? How does he treat his friends? Does he ever skip breakfast? Would he help you move furniture into your new cave or would he say that he had a nagging horn injury?"

Charlie had to find a way to keep his hands performing the movements Beeon had shown, chant the words written in the spell book and manage to ignore everything that Beeon was saying.

Charlie had no intention of reaching out to a triceratops who skipped breakfasts in order to gorge himself during a meal he called lunkfast (brunch wouldn't be invented for another 65 million years). No, Charlie fixed his mind instead on the only dinosaur who could provide the answers he sought, the only dinosaur other than Beeon who was there when whatever happened happened. Charlie thought of the corythosaurus they called Occidor.

He pictured Occidor clearly and then he went deeper. He thought of Occidor's muted, almost nonexistent response to the news of the meteor. What did it say about him that he was unfazed at the thought of their society being thrown into chaos and destruction?

Charlie thought of how Occidor had acted as he walked amongst the other dinosorcerers practicing in the field of apple trees. There was a look in his eye – was it…jealousy – a feeling that he could do as much or more than the others but something was holding him back. And Charlie remembered how he had looked at Beeon, in particular – younger and already more trusted by their master.

Just then Charlie thought, "Oh, no."

A mist had begun to form in the space between Charlie and Beeon. Within the mist, a form was starting to take shape. It solidified into a tail, then legs from which bloomed a wide scaly body.

Beeon continued to chant as he stared in astonishment at the figure beginning to materialize before him.

"Beeon, I think I made a mistake," Charlie shouted. Charlie stopped chanting but he had lost control over his hands which continued to sweep the air.

Beeon hadn't heard Charlie preoccupied as he was with the success of the spell but as the mist continued to take shape and revealed itself to be bipedal – standing on just two legs - Beeon glanced over at Charlie with some concern realizing that his apprentice hadn't strictly followed his instructions.

"Charlie, did you misunderstand me?"

"No," Charlie confessed.

Now the neck was stretching out from its body. As a head began to sprout from the neck, a look of dawning alarm crossed Beeon's face and he dove across the cave tackling Charlie and rolling with the boy in his arms behind a table. Beeon pushed a finger to his flat lips to indicate that Charlie needed to remain silent.

From under the table, Charlie saw a tail and wide, taloned feet more solid than the mist but still not quite "there." The ghostly corythosaurus took a few tentative steps around the cave, testing his new body. The feet passed close enough to the table for Charlie to notice the scratches and nicks in his toe claws.

Charlie and Beeon were frozen in place. They heard a sniffing noise like a dog searching out a scent. Then, from right above them, came a low growl: "Hello, Beeon. What took you so long?"

CHAPTER ELEVEN

Still crouched under a table, Beeon made a series of gestures to Charlie that indicated "stay quiet," "be careful" and "don't move." Charlie replied with a thumbs up that indicated "I wouldn't dream of it."

Beeon's thumb spikes were stuck in a permanent thumbs up so he simply nodded in response.

Diving across the room and rolling over the cave floor seemed to have taken a toll on Beeon. He stood very slowly, leaning on objects around him for support. "Hello, Occidor," Beeon said stifling a groan.

Charlie wanted to obey Beeon's requests including "don't move" but he needed to scoot himself into a position where he could see the two dinosorcerers. He managed to peek around one of the benches set at the table to gain a clearer view.

Occidor and Beeon stood facing each other. Occidor looked young and strong, somehow. Beeon looked old and frail.

Occidor held his ghostly hands out in front of him,

considering them. "This is interesting," he said. "Something you created?"

"Yes, with a great deal of effort and time."

"What would you know of effort," Occidor snapped back. "You have the book. Can you imagine what I would have accomplished by now – the type of sorcerer I could have become if I had that book?"

"Quintus could. And I daresay that's why he kept it away from you."

"Perhaps, perhaps. I don't see it that way. I see an old fool who was afraid. Proud and afraid of being bested, becoming obsolete."

"You really didn't know him well, did you?"

"I know you, Beeon. Even now. I knew that you were out there somewhere. And I knew that we'd be seeing each other again. But I must admit that this," and again he held up a phantom hand, "is unexpected. I never would have guessed you'd – wait, who is that?"

Charlie froze.

Occidor was looking directly at the table where he was hiding. "An assistant? Now, now, there's nothing to fear. Please show yourself. For I know that Beeon here would never have chosen to conjure me over, say, any other dinosorcer alive. Therefore it must be you that I have to thank for this most welcome reunion."

Charlie could see no point in hiding any longer; he'd been spotted. He climbed out from behind the bench and stepped forward into the light. Occidor flinched and retreated several steps away from Charlie.

Even though the connection was no more real than a sort of magical telephone call – Occidor could not touch them and they couldn't touch him – Occidor was putting distance

50

between himself and Charlie.

"Beeon, what is that?" Occidor asked in horror. Charlie looked behind himself to see what Occidor was talking about. "Beeon, did you – is this one of your creations?"

Charlie suddenly realized that for the past 65 million years, Occidor had been living somewhere other than Earth. He'd never seen a human being. And Charlie thought he might use that to his advantage.

"I'm no magical creation. I'm a human, homo sapien," Charlie said striding briskly toward Occidor.

Beeon noticed the change in Charlie's tone, the way he was charging forward and began quickly moving his hands, undoing the spell. "I think it's time you go now, Occidor," Beeon blurted out.

Charlie continued, "And there are more of us humans, lots more. Dinosaurs aren't in charge anymore."

Beeon frantically twisted the air. Occidor's form began to dissolve once again into mist.

"If you even think of coming back here to Earth or bothering my friend ever again," Charlie said, "you'll have me and six billion other humans to deal with."

Upon Occidor's vanishing face the look of confusion and fear turned to one of pure, fierce hatred. He glared at Beeon. "You allowed them to take over our planet?" His body had disappeared – only a shapeless cloud remained – and yet Occidor's voice delivered one last message: "The time of humans has come to an end. We will be back and the Earth will be ours again."

Once the last echo of Occidor's voice had faded from the cave, Beeon began hobbling around righting the bench and mugs that had been overturned when he tackled Charlie. He closed the spell book with a sort of practiced ritual and returned it to its shelf. All the while he did this, he made a point of not looking at or speaking to Charlie.

Charlie was unsure whether Beeon was angry at him for conjuring Occidor or if he was trying to process everything that had happened but, either way, he thought it was best to leave him to it.

Finally when Beeon couldn't find a single inch of the cave left to clean, he spoke: "I think you should be getting home now." Beeon returned to his seat before the fire.

"Ok," Charlie said hesitantly. "Should I come back tomorrow? Can I help you any more?"

"No," Beeon snapped, staring intently into the fire. "I don't want you to help any more."

Charlie made his way out of the cave and crossed the quiet playground under a setting sun the color of candle flame. He wondered if his mother would ask where he'd been and what he would tell her but when he arrived home, she didn't ask.

Charlie was just in time for dinner so they sat and ate and his father talked about work. Charlie felt himself swept up in the normalcy of it all and nearly forgot everything that had happened with Beeon and the dinosorcerers.

It was only after he'd brushed his teeth and laid down in bed that those words came back to him: "We will be back and the Earth will be ours again."

It didn't sound good. But what could he do?

CHAPTER TWELVE

For the second day in a row, Charlie sat in his classroom his mind buzzing with thoughts and none of them school work.

He wished he could go back to that moment when Beeon asked him to help with the spell. Why didn't he choose a different dinosaur – any other dinosaur?

Maybe everything would be okay. Maybe Beeon could hold Occidor off by himself. No, Occidor had gotten stronger over the past 65 million years while Beeon had grown older, weaker and more forgetful. Charlie had to do something to help but Beeon wouldn't accept Charlie's help anymore.

As this cyclone of thoughts whipped through Charlie's mind, he heard a soft voice calling to him: "Charlie, Charlie." The voice seemed as if it were miles away or just three feet to his right. Charlie decided to check to his right and there he found his friend, Meredith, whisper-shouting to get his attention.

Charlie, emerging from his haze, noticed that the classroom was unnatural quiet. Not even their teacher Mr.

53

Howell was speaking. Now that she had his attention, Meredith began to mime to Charlie. She pointed to Charlie; translation: "Charlie, I have something important to tell you."

She pointed to her bare wrist; translation: "I'm thinking I should look into buying a watch." Couldn't she have saved this for the playground?

Finally, she pointed to his desk; translation: "You should really take a look down at your desk. There you'll find a test that you haven't started and is due in five minutes." Gah! Why did she waste Charlie's time with that watch nonsense?

Ok, focus, Charlie. You can finish this 10-page test in the next five minutes and figure out how to stop the dinosaurs coming to wipe out the human race later.

Astronomy, good, Charlie thought, *I occasionally pay attention during astronomy*. He began racing through the columns of questions, circling "C"s at a frenzied pace and then, in the middle of the third page, there it was. Right there in the last place he would have expected to find it was useful information. Just seven small dots on a photocopier-grey page, but to Charlie, it was the missing piece to a puzzle he'd been confounded by since yesterday afternoon.

"This is it. This is the answer," Charlie shouted.

"Mr. Appleday," Mr. Howell said from the front of the room, "while I'm sure it is a very fine answer, I'd ask that you keep your answers to yourself." The class laughed. Meredith buried her head under her test pages.

"Sorry, Mr. H. Sometimes I can't contain my love for astronomy." Charlie rushed through the rest of the test, circling the final answer as Mr. Howell was pulling the paper out from under his pencil.

The school bell rang and students began to shuffle off to

their next class. Meredith cornered Charlie just outside the classroom door. "What is wrong with you? We were supposed to hang out yesterday after school and you never showed up. You've been in a daze all morning and now that performance in science class," she said. "I have come to expect a certain level of weirdness from you but this is almost too much."

"How far away from us is the big dipper?" Charlie asked distractedly.

"You're looking for answers to the test now? It's too late."

"Not the test. This is for something else. How far?"

"They're seven stars and each one is a different distance," she sighed. "On average," Meredith did some very quick math in her head. "2.9 million light years."

"Great," Charlie said, gathering his books. "See you later."

"Wait a minute." Meredith chased him out into the hallway. "You're not even going to try to explain yourself?"

"You're right," Charlie said. "That wasn't fair. Meet me at the park after school."

He started to walk away then turned back. "Listen, I know it seems like I've been acting weird; that's why I didn't mention the dinosaur wizards coming to conquer the Earth. So...see you later."

CHAPTER THIRTEEN

"This was a bad idea…(bad idea)…." Meredith said.

"Which part…(part)…((part))?" Charlie asked.

"All of it. The part where I didn't run in the opposite direction when you mentioned dinosaur wizards. The part where I agreed to meet you after school and now the part where we're crawling through a cave…(cave)…((cave))."

"Had to be done. This is where he lives. But keep it down," Charlie whispered to eliminate the echo. "He's very angry with me at the moment,"

"Should we be sneaking up on him then?"

Charlie responded by pressing a finger to his lips to indicate, "I'd rather not answer that so let's be quiet now." They moved on through the cave in quiet and dark.

As they approached Beeon's chamber, Charlie remembered the humming he heard yesterday from outside the cave and couldn't help feeling disconcerted by its absence. Had Beeon heard them coming? Was he lying in wait?

"Are we almost there?" Meredith whispered.

"Yes," Charlie said and added much later. "I think so." He remembered basically all of the important turns and climbs to take to get to Beeon's chamber but it did seem to be taking longer than he'd expected.

As they rounded what must have been the fifth or sixth left turn, they discovered a glow coming from the tunnel in front of them – a green light hovering a few feet off the ground. It was not bright enough to be the candles of Beeon's chamber but it was a light and that was a welcome break from the darkness. They approached cautiously.

When they were just a few feet away and the glow appeared the size and shape of a manhole cover, jets of green light shot out of the central light source illuminating the cave walls and revealing the glow to be a liquid bubbling gently in an enormous black cauldron.

A woman's face emerged from the darkness behind the cauldron cast in the green light swirling around the cave. They saw a sharp, warty nose; long, matted hair; and clacking teeth. She reached out to them with fingers like winter branches. "Just the ingredients I needed to finish my stew," the woman said and laughed a cackling laugh.

Meredith screamed and turned to run. But Charlie didn't move. "Wait," he said. "It's not real. Witches aren't real."

"You believe in dinosorcerers," Meredith shouted.

"This is different. It's some kind of test, a security system maybe," Charlie said.

The witch crept closer her eyes shining with malice. If Charlie had to rate his confidence that this was not a real witch, he'd put it at about 67%...maybe 70%. But even if she was just a sort of magical car alarm, he wasn't as confident that she couldn't do him some kind of harm. And she was getting closer.

"If it's a security system, it must have a password," Meredith yelled from behind Charlie.

The witch had backed Charlie into a notch in the cave wall. "Yes. A password. That's it." The witch lifted her arms jerkily like a marionette, her hands curled into claws.

"But it would have to be something Beeon wouldn't forget." Charlie thought for a moment. "He forgets everything. What does that leave?" The witch was so close now that Charlie could feel her breath pouring out from between those black teeth.

"Quintus," Charlie spoke tentatively but the witch pressed on. She lunged and grabbed his arms. Her gnarled fingernails, sharp as needles, sank into the flesh of his arms and Charlie's confidence level was plummeting.

"Occidor," Charlie shouted. "Occidor."

The witch exploded into swirling clouds of green light. Then the light and the cauldron dissolved into mist revealing the entrance to Beeon's chamber.

"Nice work," Meredith said.

"Thanks but don't let your guard down. There might be more surprises. He was pretty mad yesterday."

Meredith walked behind Charlie as he entered the chamber. "Beeon?" Charlie called. "I'm sorry about yesterday. I want to talk. I think I have some information."

The chamber was quiet. Charlie and Meredith carefully looked into alcoves, behind furniture, but the chamber seemed to be empty. "Maybe he set up the witch because he was going out, like locking your door before you leave," Meredith suggested.

"I think you're right," Charlie agreed. "It doesn't look like he's here."

"So...what do we do now?" she asked.

"We could wait."

"But you don't know where he went or when he'll be back?"

"No," Charlie said glumly.

Since last night Charlie had thought over and over about how he had been wrong to misuse Beeon's spell, to seek out answers selfishly and to disregard Beeon's wishes. It was foolish and reckless and might have endangered all of mankind.

But then again, he'd only done it because he couldn't get those answers the easier and harmless way. He had respected Beeon's feelings about revisiting painful memories. But now, Beeon wasn't around. And Charlie didn't want Meredith to have come all this way only to see a fake (but terrifying) witch.

"Meredith," Charlie asked, "did you ever wonder what 65 million years ago was like?"

CHAPTER FOURTEEN

Charlie scanned through the shelves of potions. He tried to remember the shape of the vial and the distinct hue of the potion Beeon had used yesterday. He arrived at one, finally, that he was reasonably sure was correct.

"Ok, we're going to drink this and we'll travel back to the moment the meteor hit Earth and started the dinosaurs' extinction. We'll finally know what happened," Charlie explained.

Meredith glanced sidelong at the vial in Charlie's hand. "Do you have a cup?"

"No. Why?"

"I have to drink from that vial after you?"

"You can go first if that makes you feel better," Charlie said, exasperated.

"But you drank out of it yesterday."

Charlie stretched his sleeve over his hand and used it to thoroughly wipe the lip of the vial. "Better?"

"I guess." Meredith took the vial and drank. Charlie wiped it clean again and drank too.

They stood facing each other in the quiet cave. "What happens now?" Meredith asked.

"Now we travel back in Beeon's unreliable memory to the day the dinosorcerers escaped Earth. Something strange happened and Beeon won't talk about it. We're going back to see for ourselves. It might be the key to understanding and defeating Occidor."

"So you can visit his memories without him here?"

"Oh," Charlie hadn't considered this. Would the potion work without the owner of the memories present? "No, now that you mention it, I'm not sure I can."

While they were talking, a long, ominous crack had formed across the ceiling of the cave. The walls shook and shards of crystal rained down from the roof of the cave. Like watching an egg cracked open from the inside, Charlie and Meredith looked up to see the fissure in the cave ceiling tremble, then split wide open.

However, in the absence of a guiding memory, what greeted them was not a sunny blue Jurassic sky but a blackness. Not like the night sky full of stars and a white marshmallow moon, it was pure, endless blackness and it was spreading.

"Do something, Charlie," Meredith urged. The cave had grown very cold. The candles and fireplace had all been extinguished by the dark vacuum sucking air out of the cave.

"It can't find the memory we're looking for. We're headed for nothingness," Charlie said. "We need someone who was there. We need Beeon."

"Find someone else," Meredith shouted over a howling wind.

Someone else? Everyone else who had been there was extinct or transported to a distant realm. All out of

61

someones, Charlie began to look for something. Something here must have been with Beeon back then. Would it be enough to anchor them to that time, Charlie wondered? It was worth a shot.

Charlie frantically scanned the room. Did the stool look 65 million years old? Beeon's robe had a "Coleman" label and looked like a repurposed camping tarp. And then he saw it: Quintus' book nestled in its special spot on the bookcase.

Charlie ran toward the bookcase but the cave floor was sinking under his feet like quicksand. His legs churned desperately. Deep cracks had formed in the cave wall that held the bookcase. It was beginning to collapse in on itself.

Charlie scrambled up on Beeon's crumbling table to get some solid footing, stepping over loose candy wrappers and half empty vials. Charlie leapt toward the bookcase with the last bit of strength in his legs. If he missed, he would land on a floor that wasn't there anymore, just blackness and a long way down. He reached, closed his eyes, stretched toward the spot where the book had been and hoped.

CHAPTER FIFTEEN

"How long are you going to hug that thing?"

Charlie opened his eyes to see Meredith standing over him against a patch of blue sky. He was clutching Quintus' book to his chest and lying on his back in the grass.

"It worked?" Charlie released the book and jumped to his feet.

"I think it worked. At least according to that," Meredith pointed Charlie's attention to the sky where a huge rock surrounded by churning grey clouds hung in the sky. It looked like the moon through a telescope, covered in rocks in craters. Unfortunately Charlie was seeing all that detail with his naked eyes. It appeared to be barely moving but Charlie and Meredith knew that it was in fact approaching them at a tremendous speed.

"Now that we've made it here, are you sure you can get us out of here before…." Meredith traced a falling arc with her finger, brought her hands together and made them explode outward. "Kaboosh?"

"Yeah, I think so. Anyway, we're not ready for that yet."

Charlie looked reflexively for his anchor to this time period but the ground around his feet was empty. "The book, it's gone!"

"You just set it down," Meredith said. "It's got to be here."

"I know - wait. When I came here with Beeon, he became part of the memory. He was young; he was a student dinosorcerer again. The book must have done the same thing. It can't be with us because that's not where it should be right now."

"But where is it then?"

"I don't know," Charlie said. "But I think we should follow them." He pointed behind Meredith where a line of dinosaurs, dozens of them, was marching single-file with robotic, synchronized steps.

"Is that...are those…" Meredith goggled to see living, breathing dinosaurs kicking up clouds of dirt, shaking the ground with their steps.

"Those are just plain, everyday dinosaurs," Charlie replied. "You see that one at the front? She's walking backwards, concentrating on maintaining her hypnosis spell. That's a dinosorcerer. Tregdar, I believe."

Meredith and Charlie followed the line of marching dinosaurs as it wound through the dusty valley. Along the way, they saw dinosorcerers putting into practice the spells that Quintus had taught them.

Unable to deny the truth of Quintus' predictions any longer, the local dinosaur tribes had erupted into panic and chaos. A stampeding mob of apatosaurs came charging through a cut in the rocks. A pair of young styracosaurs who had fallen too far behind their herd were caught in the path of the rampaging giants. They squeaked out calls of help;

their little legs unable to carry them quickly enough to avoid disaster. Just then, a member of the styracosaurus herd stood, rising over the others, hands slicing through the air and a strong, solid bubble appeared around the styracosaurus children. Apatosaurs stomped on or stumbled over the bubble but the youngsters inside were safe.

Charlie and Meredith looked up to see a pteranodon swooping over the valley. Each time it dove, the pteranodon latched on to one or two of the small boulders lying scattered about the valley floor. The rocks hung just below the pteranodon's taloned feet as it flew off into the distance and dropped them in a pile before circling back to collect more boulders. Soon, the tower of rocks stood as tall as a skyscraper.

"What is that thing it's building?" Charlie asked. "Doesn't seem like a great time for construction projects."

"It's amazing. Don't you see?" Meredith said. "It's a beacon."

Sure enough, dinosaurs who had moments before been running in every direction gripped by confusion and fear began instinctively moving toward the tower. As they drew closer to the base of the tower, the crowd of dinosaurs grew thicker. They were less frenzied now, thanks in some cases to a hypnotism spell, but still uneasy. They were waiting but didn't know for what and the rock in the sky had grown huge and cast a widening shadow over the entire valley.

"There," Meredith shouted. Charlie followed her pointing finger and saw the book. It was clutched in the hands of a young, nervous Beeon standing next to Quintus and trailed by Occidor.

CHAPTER SIXTEEN

Charlie and Meredith cut through the crowd of dinosaurs, ducking swinging tails, dodging heavy feet, taking a shortcut up the neck of a stegosaurus and sliding down its back careful to hop off before the spikes. They were making their way toward the book.

As they approached the front of the crowd, they saw Quintus surrounded by his dinosorcerers. "You've done very well today," Quintus said. "It looks as if you have collected everyone in the direct impact zone. But our work has just begun. In the coming weeks, the world will be blanketed by dust and debris. We will return here and begin the task of finding or creating sources of food and heat for dinosaurs across the planet. We will rebuild. It will not be easy but I know that all of us, working together, will be up to the challenge."

"Now I will open the gate," Quintus continued. "I would like all of you to lead the way. It will reassure the others. I will remain here with Beeon and Occidor until every dinosaur has entered the gate. Thank you, dinosorcerers.

You've made me very proud today."

He motioned to Beeon and Beeon stepped toward him holding the book high. Quintus opened the book, found his page and began casting the spell. His hands whirled; the portal opened. The crowd seemed to gasp as one when the blue window appeared.

Quintus was concentrating too intently to speak so one of the oldest of his students addressed the crowd. "Through this gate you will find safety. I know that it may seem frightening but you cannot stay here. We will take you away from this place and when the conditions are right, we will bring you back. Please, follow us to save your own lives and the lives of your children."

Quintus' students began to climb through the gate. The crowd still hesitated. Dinosaurs checked the sky to remind themselves of the threat they were facing, then looked back at the portal formed by wavering blue light that lead...somewhere? They were weighing their options.

Even those who had been brought here under magical hypnosis were released now. Quintus had made it clear: everyone needed to make this choice of their own free will. While the dinosaurs nearest the portal were milling about nervously looking to friends or relatives for some indication of what they should do, one tall, broad allosaur pushed his way through the crowd.

"I don't think much of magic," the allosaur spoke. "And I was awfully unkind to Quintus when he tried to warn us about what was coming. But everything he said has come true. I think we owe him an apology and we owe him our trust." The allosaur turned, ducked and vanished into the portal. His wife and children stepped through right behind him. After them, an ornithomimus approached, apologized quickly to Quintus and entered the portal.

Rocks the size of basketballs were breaking away from the larger meteorite and raining down all around the valley. Any lingering uncertainty vanished and the crowd lined up to file into the portal.

The line moved slowly, particularly when a sauropod had to find a way to fit herself inside. Backing in, they found, worked better than headfirst. But it took an unusually large seismosaur getting stuck halfway in and needing a team – one group pulling from the front and another pushing from behind – before they reached this conclusion.

As the line slowly dwindled and while the impact blasts from smaller rocks grew more frequent around them, Charlie studied Quintus, Beeon and Occidor. Beeon had been put in charge of keeping the book. He held it high. He turned pages at his master's request. Quintus seemed not only to be using the page that contained the portal spell. He was calling upon a number of supplementary spells to boost his endurance under the stress of maintaining the portal for so long and occasionally throwing up a shield against a shower of debris caused by the falling rocks.

Through all this, Occidor sulked. He lent a hand to young or elderly dinosaurs who needed assistance stepping through the portal but mostly he stood watching and flinching from every rock blast.

As the process wore on, Beeon did more than just hold the book or turn pages. Quintus was beginning to fade. "Turn to 317, please," Quintus said, his voice little more than a whisper. His shoulders slumped.

"Quintus, are you alright?"

"Yes, this spell should help…." He began to chant the words from the book but he stuttered and slurred. The portal wobbled sickeningly and the velociraptor mother handing her eggs through to the other side shrieked.

"Haukash, thoghnah…" Beeon spoke the words, clearly, loudly. Quintus' hands had fallen to his sides. They suddenly snapped back into motion. Beeon's spell propped Quintus up but left him looking slightly stiff, like a scarecrow. A deep weariness still showed in his eyes.

"Thank you, Beeon. Not much longer." The last dinosaurs in line were standing before the portal now.

"Beeon, you may go," Quintus said when the last dinosaur had entered the portal. "You're no longer needed." Beeon folded the book and stepped toward the portal. It had begun to flicker again around the edges.

Beeon turned, worry written across his face. "How will you keep it open and pass through?"

"I'll be fine, Beeon. Please, go."

Standing at the portal, Beeon cast one, final glance back to Quintus. A ball of fire came screaming over Charlie's head. He could almost feel the heat of it. It would have hit Quintus directly in the chest but Beeon, one foot through the gate, raised his hands, dropped the book and tossed up a weak magical shield. When the flaming rock collided with it, the shield shattered instantly.

The force of the impact blasted Beeon through the portal away from earth. The rock hit Quintus in the shoulder slowed only slightly and deflected off course by Beeon's shield. Quintus crumpled to the ground.

Occidor was trembling with fear and rage. He scooped the book off of the ground and dashed to his master's side. "Are you trying to kill me?" Occidor screamed. "Why did you keep me here, old man?"

"You've been under my protection; you were perfectly

safe," Quintus said. "But to answer your question, I needed to ensure there would be no 'accidents.'"

"Very clever. But I was helping us," Occidor sneered. "Why save them all? We could have started clean, without any of their backward beliefs and fears. A new society of pure science, pure reason."

"Pure hatred. I will not allow anyone to endure suffering I might have prevented."

"I suppose you believed that speech he gave - that they respect you now? As soon as they get comfortable again they'll start to fear and despise what we can do."

"Not 'we,' Occidor. Your education has ended. I tried. I hoped that with time and my guidance you would avoid this path but you resisted everyone who tried to help you. Go and join the others but never again call yourself a dinosorcerer."

"Arrogant right to the end, old timer. You think you choose who is or isn't a dinosorcerer? Who were you to decide who was worthy and dole out information as you saw fit? Who gave you that power?" He shook with a barely contained rage. "Well, no more. See, this," he waved the book in Quintus' face. "I've got it now and I'll decide who's worthy of reading it. Goodbye, Quintus."

As Occidor turned toward the shrinking portal, he let out a great 'oof' and the book soared out of his hands. He toppled over backwards. It looked like the portal had suddenly become solid and he'd slammed right into it. But, no, it was something else. He had collided with something coming through the portal in the other direction.

The valley lay fully engulfed in the shadow of the incoming meteorite now. It was difficult for Charlie and Meredith to see much more than a dark shape emerging from the portal but when a ball of flaming rock streaked past and landed 10 feet away from them throwing up a fountain of sparks, Charlie saw Beeon had returned from the other side.

"Beeon, leave here now," Quintus shouted with the last of his strength. Beeon and Occidor both dove for the book. The book came open and Occidor wound up with one end in his hands while Beeon held the other. They each pulled desperately in opposite directions. The book's spine creaked, ready to split.

Another explosion rocked the ground nearby and Occidor flinched instinctively. The book slipped from his grip and he was left holding only a page. The page slowly detached from the book and Occidor's momentum sent him reeling backwards. He stumbled, tripped and fell, arms flailing, into the portal. It was collapsing around him. His tail disappeared inside just as the portal shrunk to the size of an apple and then blinked out of existence.

Beeon ran to his master. "Beeon, you shouldn't have come back. There are only minutes left."

The meteor was so close now it filled the sky with an ambient roar like an endless thunder coming from all around them. Heavy winds whipped and swirled around the valley and the rock blasts were constant now. "I just need to find shelter where I can cast spells. I'll protect you. I'll heal you," Beeon said.

"My cave," Quintus groaned. All the magic they'd cast to boost his strength was leaving him. He seemed almost to be withering before their eyes. Beeon cast a quick spell to lift and move Quintus carrying him back toward his cave, the spell book tucked under one arm. Charlie and Meredith followed.

"Are you sure this is safe?" Meredith shouted over the

wind, the roar of the meteor and rocks falling all around them.

"I think so," Charlie said. "This is only the second time I've done it and things weren't exploding last time."

They all reached the cave and Beeon set Quintus gently down on his bed of leaves and straw. They were free of the winds and falling rocks but the swelling sound of the incoming meteor reminded them that they were far from safe, even in here.

Beeon flipped through the spellbook furiously. "Spell of wakefulness? No, it has to be stronger. Soothe an upset stomach? Where are the real healing spells…."

"There is nothing in that book that can help me now," Quintus said his voice barely a whisper. "You shouldn't have come back. I think you might've been one of the best of us. You might have done so much good…." His eyes closed.

Beeon returned to the book and began speaking any words he could read through his tears. He started spells and flipped to another before he finished, no time to read their effects. The air around him began to glow but Quintus remained still.

"I can save you. I just need more time…."

Just then there was an explosion like nothing Charlie had ever heard before. The sound had a weight and a power. It knocked the three of them – Charlie and Meredith and Beeon – off their feet. The ground heaved and bucked tossing them about like ocean waves. From above them came a whine and a crack and, just in time, Beeon had created a magic bubble as the cave roof collapsed.

He was straining and fighting to concentrate as he continued to look to the book for something that could help Quintus. The bubble flickered and as debris continued to pelt down, it sounded like it was raining bowling balls above them. Beeon's arms shook and he screamed then the bubble burst and everything went black.

CHAPTER SEVENTEEN

Charlie couldn't tell if he was moving or standing still. All he saw was pure blackness. He tried to walk but he couldn't see or feel his feet.

He tried to shout to Meredith to ask if she was okay but he couldn't hear his own voice.

He waited.

Charlie wasn't good at waiting. Pretty quickly, he went back to shouting. And when he finally heard a voice – not his own but a voice nonetheless – that cut through the endless, silent dark, it felt like the sweetest sound he'd ever heard.

"Are you satisfied now?" Beeon's voice boomed all around him. "I can bring you back...unless you want to continue digging through my memories."

"No," Charlie tried to say but still no sound. He shook his head. He didn't know if any of this was reaching Beeon. He wanted badly to explain why they were here but he didn't know if Beeon would allow him the chance.

Suddenly, a halo of light appeared above him. Charlie floated toward it as if resurfacing from deep underwater. As he drew nearer, the halo grew and spread and the darkness faded. Finally, Charlie found himself lying on the cave floor looking up at the candles that ringed the room. He glanced to his right and saw Meredith lying a few feet away, blinking, breathing, and clearly in a state of shock.

Beeon stood in the corner, his back to them, replacing the spell book in its spot on the shelf. "So now you understand...I wasn't strong enough."

Charlie pushed himself up to his feet. "You were only a kid. There was nothing you could do." He helped Meredith to her feet and then into a chair.

"No," Beeon said. "I could have protected him. I could have saved him and together we could have helped the others. But I was unconscious for days after the cave collapsed. It was nearly a week before I emerged from the rubble and by then...it was too late. Everything, everyone I knew was extinct or somewhere so far away I thought I'd never see them again. That was a memory I did not wish to revisit. So, now, Charlie and Miss…."

"M - Meredith." Still glassy-eyed, she seemed to be emerging from her stupor.

"Charlie and Meredith, please leave."

"But we came for a reason," Charlie started. "We -"

"Wanted to know what happened at the end, yes, and now you can go," Beeon cut him off.

"No, listen, we need to tell you – we might know where they are, the rest of your kind, the survivors."

Beeon considered the word for a long moment: survivors. Living dinosaurs like himself. The thought of a companionship he hadn't experienced in millions of years. His brusqueness melted away in an instant. "You...know where they are?"

75

"Possibly," Charlie answered. "Now tell me, you were there briefly before you came back. What do you remember?"

Beeon closed his eyes and began to pace the room. "I was knocked backward...I landed on my back and I was blinded. I was looking straight up into the sun."

"Ok, anything else?"

"It's hazy. I'd taken a tremendous blow. I rose to my feet and saw something strange...the sun setting on the horizon. But it doesn't make sense. I couldn't have been down that long."

"No, it was just a minute or two. Keep going," Charlie encouraged.

Meredith, fully alert now, jumped up from her chair and ran to the corner where she'd set down her book bag when they came in. She found a binder full of loose lined pages and a pencil; then she returned to her seat and began jotting notes as Beeon spoke.

"Well, I realized what had happened and that Occidor and Quintus were on the other side. I had to help him so I leapt back through."

"Nothing else?"

"It's so hard to remember...but now that you mention it, I had suffered a head trauma. I was seeing double. I remember as I ran toward the portal, the sun split in two just above the rim of its opening. I'm sorry I'm so forgetful, children. I wish I could be more help."

"No, Beeon, that's perfect." Charlie looked to Meredith. "Did you get all that?"

Meredith's head was buried in her notes. She was furiously scribbling angles, calculations. "I got it. Just give me a moment."

"Beeon, let me explain." Charlie ran to the corner and fetched his science textbook from his bag. "We believe that the portal took the others somewhere around...here." He had opened to a two-page spread of the solar system and stabbed his finger right in the middle of a long stretch of uninterrupted black ink.

"What is that?"

"We're not sure what it is but I noticed something when Quintus opened the portal the first time. Not just one but several suns. And then when I was taking my science test."

"Bombing," Meredith added without looking up from her notes.

"Bombing my science test today. I saw this," he flipped a few more pages and pointed.

"The big dipper?"

"Yes. This collection of stars seen from a point much closer to them could produce what you and I saw."

"Can you say how much closer – exactly?" Beeon asked.

"That's where I come in." Meredith stood, tucked her pencil behind her ear and set her notes in front of Charlie and Beeon on the table. "Based on their angle of ascension and relative size in the sky, we can determine that the planet they were viewed from must lie approximately 2.6 light years from Phecda, the lower tip of the big dipper's spoon. Or you can think of it as 72 light years away from earth."

She flipped the paper over, drew a small circle and wrote "earth" inside. She began drawing a map, labeling points of interest along the way (Saturn, Orion's belt, dogstar) as if she were giving directions to a friend's birthday party. "The planet you're looking for is right...here."

Beeon stared at the page and traced the map with the first finger on one lightly shaking hand. "Children, this is

77

astounding. With this, I might be able to find the others and warn them. They can help me stop Occidor. I can't thank you enough. I couldn't have done this without you. But now…you should be going."

"What are you talking about?" Charlie whined. "We gave you the map. Now you need to open the portal. We want to see it."

"Your help has been invaluable," Beeon said, "but I don't believe you can be of any more assistance."

"We can't even peek inside?"

"No," Beeon whipped his head side to side in an emphatic denial. "It is too dangerous."

"I agree with Beeon," Meredith said. "We were just very nearly killed and that was just a memory. A land of living dinosaurs, many of whom know magic, some of whom have pledged their allegiance to an angry maniac? No thanks."

Charlie gave Meredith a wounded look. Couldn't she hear how imminently cool everything she just described sounded?

"Well, we should at least watch you open the portal in case Meredith miscalculated anything."

"I didn't mis-"

Charlie leaned close to her and hissed, "Just give me this much, okay?"

"Sure," Meredith agreed. "Maybe I miscalculated something."

Beeon's face broke into a wide, sly smile and it felt to Charlie like something he'd lost and only realized how much he missed it now that it was found. "Yes, I suppose you do deserve just a small look inside but then you really must go."

"Of course. One look and we go," Charlie's grin was so wide it looked almost painful and Meredith suspected he might be lying.

"We certainly wouldn't want to stay too long," Charlie said. "With all of this science and math talk, I can't wait to get home and dig into my homework."

Now she knew he was lying.

CHAPTER EIGHTEEN

Beeon had arranged the spell book and map on the table in front of him. He cracked his knuckles and ran through a series of exercises intended to loosen up his finger and wrists. Beeon began chanting softly. His voice echoed around the chamber. He stared at the map Meredith had drawn and manipulated the air with his fingers.

"You are sure about those calculations, right?" Charlie whispered to Meredith.

"Of course I am. It is simple advanced trigonometry," Meredith said. "Why do you ask?"

"Well, if you were off by half a mile – next to nothing when you're calculating light years of space – he would be opening a portal not to the dinosaur planet but to empty space. I think you and I both know that space is a vacuum and a portal opened there would suck us all out into a cold oxygen-less void."

Meredith looked to the ceiling frantically applying Pythagoras' Theorem. "I'm pretty sure," she said finally. "And what about you? Are you sure about the big dipper? It could have been any collection of stars."

"I know what I saw," Charlie said. "At least I'm pretty sure."

"Ok, we're agreed then. We're both pretty sure."

The blue box had started to form in the air and Charlie didn't feel himself being pulled toward it. That was a good sign.

The box grew and soon the light from the other side was spilling across the cave floor. Beeon remained focused until the portal had grown tall enough to allow him through. Charlie approached the portal and looked through to the other side. He saw lush green grasses and counted: one, two, three, four, five suns, with two more on the other side of the planet. Looks right.

Beeon stepped closer and stared through the portal, mouth hanging open. "Is – is that really it?"

"It sure looks like it," Meredith said.

"Thank you, children. I can return to my friends. Old Trappel, I wonder what he's been doing all these years. He must have some better jokes by now, I think. And oh, Declee...I was quite fond of her…." He trailed off losing himself in a flood of memories before he snapped back to the present. "Children, I have something I want to leave you."

Beeon shuffled off back to the table, closed the spell book and walked back holding it out in front of himself. He bowed slightly and presented it to Charlie and Meredith.

"This? We can't take this," Charlie said. "What if you need it?"

"I've had 65 million years to memorize the important ones and it's safer here with you. If I carried it, its magic would call to Occidor like a beacon. No, it must stay here and I would like you two to care for it for me. Can you do that?"

Charlie accepted the book silently.

"Goodbye, children. I will not forget you." He turned to step through the portal.

"Wait!" Charlie shouted. Beeon looked back. "Who knows where you'll end up. You could be miles away from civilization. You need to pack supplies."

"I can conjure most of what I need," Beeon protested but Charlie had already begun dumping his backpack out on the floor. Charlie pulled some bundles of fresh leaves wrapped in twine off of Beeon's shelves and stuffed them in the backpack. He found jugs of water and used them first to rinse the remnants of chicken noodle soup from his thermos then to fill the thermos with clean cool water.

"You never know," Charlie called as he flitted about the cave. "Best to be prepared."

As he passed by the table, Charlie very carefully, very secretly swept up the map Meredith had drawn and tucked it into the backpack's front pocket. And this was the real reason Charlie insisted Beeon take the backpack, because Charlie thought maybe someday he might want to come back. He couldn't really be leaving them for good. When the threat had passed, when he was ready to reward them more generously for their contribution, he would be back. And for that, he would need the map.

Charlie handed the backpack to Beeon and though the iguanodon couldn't manage to swing it over his back – his arms were too short and back too wide – with some adjusting of straps, he was able to slip it over his shoulders and across his chest.

"Goodbye, Beeon."

"Goodbye, Charlie."

"Goodbye, Beeon. I wish we'd gotten to know each other better."

"Goodbye, Meredith."

Beeon turned and stepped through the portal and the blue box contracted to the size of a postage stamp before blinking out of existence entirely. And Beeon was gone.

"Um, ok. So you can keep the book on Monday, Tuesday and Wednesday and I get it Thursday through Saturday and each Sunday is determined by a best two out of three coin flip with no one being allowed possession on more than two consecutive Sundays. Deal?"

Meredith looked at the spell book in Charlie's hands, as wide as a textbook but as thick as a dictionary and covered in what looked like flattened bark that flaked off if you handled it too roughly.

"No deal," she said. "Are you kidding? I can't bring that thing home. My little brother is constantly snooping in my room. He'd find it in about five minutes and then take it to my parents."

Charlie got excited for a second thinking that now he could keep the book full-time but then he imagined trying to sneak the book past his parents especially without a book bag. He really needed to start thinking up an excuse for losing that and the thermos.

"I've got an idea," Meredith interrupted Charlie in the midst of concocting a story about a wild bear who, driven mad by the thermos's lingering smell of chicken noodle soup, had burst from the woods and torn his backpack to pieces. "We could leave it here."

"In the cave?"

"Yes. Right on the shelf. It's been safe here for millions

of years. You and I could come visit it anytime we liked."

"Hmm, like our own clubhouse. With a book of real magic spells in it. You've convinced me. Let's do it." Charlie walked over to Beeon's shelf and replaced the book in its slot.

"So we'll meet back here tomorrow after school," Meredith said.

"Yes. And if my mom asks you, the bear was 10 feet tall. The details make it believable."

CHAPTER NINETEEN

Charlie spent fourth period dreaming about returning to the cave.

He had survived his return home the previous night. His punishment for losing his backpack was being forced to use his sister's second-grade bookbag. It was decorated in fuzzy bunnies and lollipops. Charlie tried turning it inside out but then the straps didn't work. A new thermos would be coming out of his allowance. It was worth it for the possibility of seeing Beeon again...sometime.

For now there was Beeon's book to keep him busy. Which spell should he start with? He'd already kind of done one with Beeon's help so he could probably skip the beginner stuff. Lifting things? He could take out the trash without leaving the couch. Breathe fire? Learn to fly?

"Charlie!" Meredith was whisper-shouting again. Her eyes directed Charlie toward the front of the room where Mrs. Bookman was sitting.

"Mr. Appleday, are you ready to present your creative writing assignment?"

"Creative writing?" Charlie rummaged through his sister's bookbag and pulled out a notebook that he knew did not contain last night's creative writing assignment.

There were myriad reasons the assignment would not be found in that notebook: he'd spent most of his afterschool hours opening a portal to a planet located very near to the Big Dipper; he'd burned up much of his creative energy explaining to his parents what had happened to his thermos; he had some comic book reading to catch up on. But none of those mattered now.

All that mattered was that Mrs. Bookman expected a story and Charlie strode confidently to the front of the room ready to give her one.

He took his place next to the teacher's desk and opened his notebook for effect.

"Once upon a time there was a wizard and then another wizard – that made two wizards.

"They were students under the same master but one of them chose to do good and the other to do evil. The bad wizard, he wanted something the good wizard had, a scroll that once belonged to their master and that held the key to unlocking great magical power."

"The bad wizard couldn't understand why his ambition, his ruthlessness, didn't earn him his master's favor. It made him angry."

"But the good wizard had more than ambition. He had kindness and empathy and he advanced more quickly in the master's school. This made the bad wizard even angrier. He planned to push his master into the dragon pit one night when he was feeding them. Then he would take the scroll. If the knowledge would not be given to him, he would steal it."

"The bad wizard carried out his plan. Their master was

devoured by hungry dragons. And though the good wizard couldn't stop him, he managed to flee the castle with the scroll before the bad wizard got ahold of it."

"The bad wizard searched all over the kingdom trying to find the good wizard and the scroll. He gathered followers who helped him search and enforced his evil commands."

"The good wizard grew tired of hiding and decided that he needed to confront and defeat the bad wizard. He left the scroll in the care of his two loyal apprentices and set forth to remove the bad wizard from the castle and free the kingdom of Eula but that is a tale for another day...."

Charlie shut his notebook dramatically and looked to Mrs. Bookman like an Olympic figure skater awaiting his score.

"Eh, B...minus. You can sit down, Mr. Appleday."

Charlie started to make his way back to his seat.

"But what happened to the scroll?" Andrew Cooper asked.

"It was left in the care of the two apprentices. Did you miss that part, Andy?" Charlie answered.

"But what if the henchmen came looking for it?" Brielle piped up. "What could they do? The apprentices couldn't defend it."

"Well, not hand to hand, maybe, but they — the apprentices — are very clever."

"Is it at least hidden where they wouldn't look?" Now Kevin Templeton was getting in on the act.

"It, uh, it was hidden in the wizard's house."

The whole class groaned as one.

"That's the first place they'll look." Charlie was a little surprised to realize that this comment had come from Mrs. Bookman.

Charlie's stomach sank. It occurred to him suddenly that

he needed to get back to the cave. He didn't bother sitting at his desk. He grabbed his sister's backpack and slung it over his shoulder.

"Mrs. Bookman, can I be excused?" Charlie asked. "And Meredith too?"

Of course Mrs. Bookman did not allow Charlie to be excused in the middle of class. Charlie would have to endure three more agonizing classes before the school day ended and he was set free.

The taunts about impending nuptials that he suffered for having asked to leave with Meredith were a welcome distraction from the worry gnawing at his guts.

Charlie found Meredith at her locker between classes. "Did you have to drag me into that performance?" Meredith slammed books into her locker.

"Yes. I need your help. We've got to do something with the book. You heard what they said. Occidor knows the cave. He's been there. It's not safe."

"No, I think they said the 'scroll' wasn't safe from the 'bad wizard.'"

"Don't you see, that story was about the dinosorcerers and us?"

"I got it, Charlie." She slammed the door of her locker so hard that the thin metal continued to rattle several seconds later. "You're going to have to get the book without me. I have softball practice."

She started to walk off toward her next class. "And when you get it, you can keep it."

CHAPTER TWENTY

Charlie was already out the door as the end-of-the-day school bell rang.

On the bus, he jumped into the seat behind the driver — easier to be the first one off — and as soon as its doors swung open at his stop, he leapt from the top step and started running toward far end of the soccer fields.

Charlie grumpily dispatched the witch and made his way into the cave. His eyes went immediately to the bookshelf and with a heavy sigh of relief, Charlie saw the spine of the spell book lined up right where he'd placed it the evening before.

When Charlie relaxed and his focus widened to take in the rest of the room, however, he noticed that everything outside of the bookshelf was not as it had been left. The floor was strewn with broken vials. Tables and stools were overturned. Beeon's chairs by the fireplace were smashed to bits.

"Ah, just what we needed." The voice coming from behind Charlie made him whirl around. "Another helper."

There, looming 15 feet tall, stood Occidor and on either side of him, a pair of pachycephalosaurus grinning so wide that drool dangled from their lower lips.

Occidor's pebbled skin looked like it had been polished. It shone like he was covered in diamonds and it rippled as he flexed his massive arms. He held the two pachycephalosaurs by collars around their necks, his arms straining as they lunged toward Charlie like angry dogs.

"Latos, Damos," Occidor shouted at his two henchmen. "You won't be needed any longer." He leaned closer and spoke softly first to one and then the other. They both stopped growling at once, sat on the floor and slowly closed their eyes until they looked like any of the dinosaur exhibits Charlie had seen at the museum.

Had that really been just two days ago? Charlie wished he could go back there, shake himself and convince the dinosaur-obsessed Charlie that there were many interesting things to learn about bird habitats.

"This is your work, I presume?" Occidor held up a tattered white sheet and Charlie immediately recognized the map that Meredith had drawn. "I must thank you for this. I went through a great many royal astronomers searching for this path. A path back to my home."

"Did you ever think that it wasn't that your astronomers couldn't figure it out?" Charlie asked. "It was just that they didn't want you to have it?"

"Yes, I did think of that, in fact. But I thought that the way that I dealt with those who failed me would serve as a lesson to the others. Whether they failed or whether they lied to protect their secrets, it ended the same for them all." Occidor had moved to put himself between Charlie and the exit. "Now you, I hope, will not be so foolish."

90

"Where is Beeon?"

"My men captured him. Not a thing happens on Megasauroplex without my knowing. He was going through the town trying to find his friends, allies, when one of the townspeople turned him in. Fear breeds that type of loyalty."

"If you hurt him…."

"No, not yet. He sits, unharmed, in my prison right now. And this part is funny, he got his wish to be reunited with his friends."

"He'll find a way out. He's smarter than you."

"He is *not* smarter than me." Occidor pounded the cave wall so hard that debris rained from the ceiling. "He was given advantages that I never had. Can you understand that? Having everything that is rightfully yours held just out of your reach?"

"Probably a lot of things are out of reach with those arms, am I right?" Charlie didn't know what he was doing but he hoped this would buy him some time to think. "Top shelves at the supermarket? Have you ever, in 65 million years, done a proper jumping jack?"

Charlie froze.

He'd been subtly backing away, trying to put some space between himself and Occidor but now he found he couldn't move. Occidor was chanting softly and lifting his hand. Charlie noticed with some dismay that his feet had lifted off the ground.

"I could just take it, you know. The secret I'm looking for? I could just reach into your mind and pluck it out. The trouble is, it's a messy procedure. My subjects are seldom the same afterwards. The twins back there," he gestured to the two frozen pachycephalosaurs, "they used to be my two most brilliant scientists. Until they decided to keep secrets from me."

No matter how he tried, Charlie could not will his limbs to work. Occidor raised his other hand and pointed his first finger at Charlie's head. A searing pain ripped at Charlie's forehead as if a scalpel were being drawn across it.

"Now, we've looked every secret place the old fool would try to hide the book. Do you want to tell me where it is? Or should I go in and get it?"

"You can dig around in Charlie's brain all day. But you won't find the book there either."

Charlie couldn't turn his head. It was stuck in place by Occidor's spell but he could shift his eyes where the voice had come from and there, framed by the mouth of the cave, he saw Meredith, still dressed in her softball uniform.

CHAPTER TWENTY-ONE

"Ah, another of these 'humans' that have infected my planet," Occidor growled at Meredith.

"Soon enough, when I become your king, I plan to get to know all of you much better but, of the two humans I've encountered so far, I must say that I find you extremely tiresome."

Charlie dropped to the floor as Occidor released him and turned toward Meredith. "Do not play games with me, girl."

"What games? I want to help you find it. Not all of us humans are like Charlie."

Charlie lay on the stone floor flexing his arms and fingers confirming they were back under his control.

"Most of us are thoughtful and sensible." Meredith's eyes connected with Charlie's and she gave him a look that he was sure meant something. But what he didn't know. It was the kind that she often flashed during class and it typically meant, "pay attention" or "the teacher just called on you; say, 'the square root of 81 is 9.'"

"You didn't think Beeon would leave the book out in the

open or *somewhere obvious*." Meredith emphasized these words in a way that seemed important to Charlie.

Now he understood the look.

Charlie climbed quietly to his feet behind Occidor's back and, slowly, Charlie began to edge toward the bookshelf.

"No, I didn't," Occidor replied. "That's why I searched all the places I would've hidden the book. But I suppose he wouldn't be quite so foolish as to leave it in his home either."

"Now you're getting it," Meredith said. "Nor would he leave it in the mind of such an oaf."

Charlie had reached the shelf and was gingerly sliding the book from its place and into his sister's backpack.

"I did think it unusual that Beeon would trust someone so impulsive." Occidor turned to regard Charlie as Charlie tried to lean nonchalantly against the shelf. He let the bag hang casually low near his feet.

"Now," Occidor returned his attention to Meredith, "you've told me where the book is not. Where is it?"

Charlie couldn't believe they had pulled it off. Now they just needed to find a way out of the cave and away from Occidor.

He was scanning the room for escape routes, distractions, when he noticed one of the pachycephalosaurs with his eyes wide open and staring at Charlie. How long had the pachycephalosaur been watching, Charlie wondered.

He didn't have to wonder long. The pachycephalosaur growled a low, rumbling roar and his lips curled back over his wide, flat teeth.

"Well," Meredith stammered, "it's not here so we'll need to go...um...to go...to where it is…."

Meredith hadn't noticed the pachycephalosaur beginning

to move. It rose to its feet, lowered its heavy, armored head and charged at the bookshelf. Charlie dove out of the way just in time and the stampeding pachycephalosaur rammed at full speed into the bookshelf and the cave wall behind it.

The bookshelf exploded in a shower of splintered wood and loose scraps of paper. The impact reverberated through the floor and walls of the cave.

"Latos, what are you doing?" Occidor shouted at his minion.

The crash must have woken the other pachycephalosaur because his eyes were open now and what he saw was his brother looking dazed, injured and the odd human creature standing nearby. Determined to defend his brother, the other pachycephalosaur leapt to his feet and charged.

Charlie was more prepared this time. He looked for cover and found it behind one of the huge stalagmites that grew up in spots around the cave – or was it a stalactite? It was impossible to tell, really, because they stretched from floor to ceiling like a pillar and could have sprouted from either end.

Whatever its proper name, Charlie ducked behind it as the second pachycephalosaur rushed closer.

"Damos, stop," Occidor screamed. But the pachycephalosaur couldn't hear over the sound of his own thunderous footsteps. He plowed through the stone pillar without slowing down.

Charlie looked up to see the solid stone disappear in a cloud of dust and to watch the pachycephalosaur pass right over him and into the wall beyond.

Again the cave trembled from the blast but now the ceiling was beginning to creak ominously. There was a popping sound like microwave popcorn as all around them rocks were shifting, loosening.

Charlie stood, dusted himself off and tried to regain his bearings when he heard, "Charlie! Run!"

Meredith was pointing behind him. Somehow he knew that he shouldn't stop to see what she was pointing at and yet he couldn't help himself. He turned and saw that both pachycephalosaurs had recovered and had their heads lowered, aimed right at him. How could he possibly dodge them both?

He ran, as Meredith had instructed. He ran without thinking; he just ran.

Hurdling the remains of Beeon's kitchen, however, Charlie began to wonder if what he was running towards was really any better than what he was running away from. There, at the front of the cave, stood Occidor awaiting Charlie, arms wide, his fingers like claws ready to snatch Charlie up.

The pachycephalosaurs were gaining on Charlie. They had longer legs and simply ran through obstacles rather than over or around them.

Charlie didn't know whether Occidor had guessed at what he carried in his sister's backpack or whether he simply wanted to stop his henchmen from causing any more accidental damage and would give them their toy once he caught it for them. Either way, Charlie needed to stay away from him.

The pachychephalosaurs were still barreling toward him but now Charlie couldn't be sure whether they were pursuing him or fleeing. Behind them, the shifting rocks had finally let go and starting at the back wall, the crystalline ceiling above them had begun to collapse.

Each step Charlie took brought him closer to Occidor. Charlie was just feet away, close enough for the dinosaur to reach down and pluck him up, when Meredith suddenly remembered her softball practice. She called to him: "Charlie, slide!"

Instincts born out of years of recess kickball games kicked in and Charlie executed the most perfect, in-under-the-tag slide he or Meredith or, presumably, the dinosaurs had ever seen.

From above him, Charlie heard Occidor bellow once again in an unsuccessful attempt to stop the charging pachycephalosaurs. He then heard a sound at once massive and muffled, like a Mack truck crashing into a pillow factory, as the first pachycephalosaur collided with Occidor's muscled frame. The sound was followed by another just like it closely after. Charlie very badly wished he could have seen all of this but he and Meredith were already running through the twisting corridor away from the cave.

They weren't far along the corridor when the faint, diminishing light coming from Beeon's cave went out like a light switch had been flipped off.

Accompanying the light going out came a sound like a heavy door being slammed shut as the cave roof gave way and sealed up the cave along with everything inside.

CHAPTER TWENTY-TWO

Charlie and Meredith both knew the layout of the tunnel system well by now and it didn't take them long to make their way out. They stood blinking in the sunlight while Charlie felt the need to confirm that the book was safely still in his backpack after all the running, jumping and sliding he'd done.

"You've got it?" Meredith asked.

"Yeah, I've got it." They both allowed themselves to catch their breath. "What about practice?"

"I realized you were right – the book wasn't safe in Beeon's cave." Charlie enjoyed a fleeting moment of satisfaction at Meredith admitting he'd been right. "And if that was true, then you were going to need my help."

"And I'm going to need your help again," Charlie said. "Can you redraw the map?"

"Yes," Meredith replied, a bit puzzled. "It shouldn't be too hard. But why?"

"It's pretty obvious, isn't it? We've got the book. You can make the map. We're going to rescue Beeon."

"Have you thought this through?" Charlie was handing her a notebook and pencil from his backpack. He clearly intended to leave immediately.

"No. I might chicken out if I did."

"Ok, at least tell me this: don't you think it will be difficult for us to blend in on a planet of dinosaurs?"

"Good point. Give me a minute. Let's see what the spell book has to say." Charlie flipped through the pages. "Mend a broken horn...no. See through boulders...that's not it. Here – alter your appearance."

"Alter how?"

"Well, it says here you can change colors, turn feathers to scales and vice versa. Quintus made a note here, 'mass can be neither created nor destroyed.'"

"65 million years before Lavoisier discovered the Law of Conservation of Mass," Meredith added.

"The point, I think, is we can't turn ourselves into sauropods or ants. It's got to be close." Charlie only needed to think for a moment. "I think I've got it. Is the map ready?"

Meredith had been drawing while Charlie scanned through spells. "Yes, but…."

"But what?"

"Are you sure?" Meredith clutched the map to her chest. "Are you sure you can change us? Are you sure you can change us back? Are you sure you can open the portal?"

"The only thing I'm sure of is that I can't leave Beeon in a prison cell. The rest of it I'm going to make up as I go along. And I hope that's enough for you because I'm also sure that I can't do any of this without your help." Charlie held out his hand for the map. "Ready now?"

Meredith loosed her grip on the map and dropped it into

Charlie's hand. "Ready."

***

"What did you turn me into?" Meredith held her scaly three-fingered hands in front of her face and spun in circles trying to get a look at her tail.

"Oryctodromeus," Charlie replied coolly. "Closest dinosaur to the size and weight of a nine-year-old kid."

Meredith was examining her now needle-sharp teeth jabbing at them with the pad of her most thumb-like finger. "These should come in handy. I wish that Occidor were here now." She snapped at the air.

As soon as he had finished with their transformations, Charlie turned his attention to the portal. It was a difficult spell and he had less fingers now. He had expected it to be a slow process of trial and error. Instead, his reptilian hands moved nimbly, almost automatically, and the spell flowed easily. Charlie felt oddly comfortable in this body and before he quite realized he'd done it, a tall door stood before them framed by a blue neon glow.

Meredith looked up. She carried a small plastic hair brush with a mirror set in its back and she'd been watching herself make faces in it. "That was fast."

"Yeah, I know."

"Part of me was hoping you wouldn't be able to do it," Meredith confessed.

"Me too."

Charlie packed the map and the book in his sister's backpack. They grasped each other's hands, took a deep breath and stepped through the portal.

100

CHAPTER TWENTY-THREE

Charlie and Meredith stepped into a field of lightly swaying grass and the portal zipped itself shut behind them. The grass, already up to their hips, seemed to grow as you watched it. There was no shade, no shadows. Every surface glowed with a golden light. Five suns will do that.

It took Charlie's eyes a moment to adjust but, when they did, he saw grass stretching to the horizon. Trees dotted the landscape, always alone, never grouped together in a forest or even a clump. Their trunks twisted like a beach towel Charlie's sister was planning to snap him with.

"Which way?" Meredith asked.

"Well, Occidor called himself an emperor. He wouldn't settle for anything less than his own castle. And he would want the dinosorcerers where he could keep an eye on them. I think they'll be in a prison there."

"Ok, but I don't see anything." She turned in a circle to emphasize that she had looked everywhere and stopped suddenly. "Wait – what's that?"

Charlie looked where Meredith indicated and saw

something rising above the leaves of grass and cutting through the rolling sea of green like a shark fin, a thin brown dagger. It was moving erratically, darting from side to side. Charlie and Meredith watched, confused and a little alarmed. They kept very still. Suddenly, it stopped weaving and headed straight for them.

"Watch out!" Charlie pushed Meredith out of the way. He had no time to move now. It was too fast. He closed his eyes with the thing just inches away from him and he felt...like someone had softly tossed a bundle of twigs at him.

Charlie opened his eyes and all he saw below him was grass. With two hands, he parted the grass and there on the ground, dazed, lay another oryctodromeus, even smaller than himself and Meredith. The little dinosaur's eyes fluttered open to see Charlie and Meredith standing over him.

"Oh, no. How did you find me?" The young oryctodromeus stood and backed away from them. "Tell the others I'm not going back home. He'll find me there and after he takes me, he'll lock up my parents for hiding me."

"Who is 'he'?" Meredith asked.

"Wait," the young oryctodromeus narrowed his eyes at them. "I haven't seen you around the village. You don't work for him, do you?" He got ready to run and his tail pointed straight up higher than the surrounding grass.

"Occidor?" Charlie asked. The oryctodromeus gave a cautious nod. "No, we don't work for him and, no, we're not from the village. We're here to help."

"Help me?" The dinosaur scoffed. "How can you help me? Do you know how to get rid of The Gift?"

"Why would you want to get rid of a gift?" Meredith asked.

"Not a gift, The Gift. The one that Occidor can smell on

you like gingko berries. The one that only comes to a special few. The one that makes Occidor take you off to his castle for 'training' but then no one ever sees you again."

"This gift," Charlie said his hands moving subtly under cover of the tall grass, "does it look anything like...this?" Charlie's beak melted away leaving only a rubbery pink nose. His tail reeled back into his body as his legs thinned and straightened. Scales softened into flesh until standing next to the dinosaur Meredith was a human Charlie.

The young oryctodromeus yelped and dropped back under the grass. A moment later his head peeked over the green stalks like a periscope. "You can do it too?" The oryctodromeus asked and without waiting for an answer followed up with: "What kind of monster did you turn yourself into?"

"It's not important," Charlie said quickly turning himself back into a dinosaur. "What's important is that we don't work for Occidor. We're here to stop him. But we need to get to his castle. Do you know where it is?"

"Of course, everyone knows where it is. But you don't want to go there. Dinosaurs with The Gift go in there and they never come out."

"Maybe we can change that," Meredith said, "with your help. Just get us there. You don't have to follow us inside."

"If our plan works," Charlie said, "you won't have to hide anymore. You won't be alone. There will be teachers who can show you how to use your gift to develop and reach your true potential."

"You — are you talking about the dinosorcerers? They're real?"

"They're real and we can find them with your help," Meredith said.

For the first time since they'd met him, Charlie and Meredith saw a smile break over the young oryctodromeus' face. "Follow me," he shouted. He disappeared below the grass again. Charlie and Meredith tried to keep up with the young dinosaur. They were amazed at the speeds they could reach in their new bodies. The landscape passed by in a blur as they followed the tip of the oryctodromeus' tail onward toward Occidor's castle.

CHAPTER TWENTY-FOUR

It started as just a bump on the horizon, a smudge. A shadow in the midst of so much golden light.

But as they kept moving, it kept growing, looming larger and larger like a black mountain. The castle seemed huge and Charlie realized they weren't even particularly close yet.

They kept running and Charlie could see that it was built from slabs of some dark stone that seemed to swallow the light. A central structure rose to a jagged peak while around it boxes and cones of irregular size had been patched on with no regard for symmetry.

Charlie as he did when he was scared, tried to make a joke. "Looks like a real DIY guy, huh?" He shouted to Meredith. "With all those additions?"

The oryctodromeus must have heard him and gotten the gist of what Charlie was saying because he shouted back, "He keeps running out of prison space. Needs to build a new one every few months." Sheesh. So much for lightening the mood.

In time they reached the outer wall of the castle. The

oryctodromeus slowed to a stop. The grass ended well before the castle walls. In a huge circle surrounding the structure, the grass faded into rocky dirt. Even with so many suns, it seemed no living thing near this place could find light enough to grow. Charlie saw no doors or windows in the structure just masses of black rock.

"Here you are," the oryctodromeus said.

"But how do we get in?" Meredith asked.

"That's a little tricky. The only way in for visitors is up there." The young oryctodromeus gestured upward to the tip of the black tower. "And you need one of the guards to bring you in. Occidor might have another way but that's the only way I've seen anyone go in."

Now that he was staring at it, Charlie could see something there at the top of the tower, a small oval opening just slightly less black than the rock around it. And around the opening perched four archeopteryx, their beaks glowing faintly in the castle's shadow.

"I don't think you want to go in that way," the oryctodromeus said.

Charlie imagined himself plucked up by the talons of the archeopteryx lifted thousands of feet off the ground and dropped down a hole in the tower. "No, I'd rather not," Charlie said.

"Luckily, I do have a plan," the oryctodromeus said. "It's crazy but…."

"No, go on."

"Well, you know The Gift I told you about?"

"Yes."

"And oryctodromeus like us are natural burrowers. My parents asked me to help with the burrow one night while they gathered some food. When they got back, our burrow

106

had 19 bedrooms, a foyer, a grand ballroom and atrium. Then we knew that something about my burrowing was...unnatural."

"Ok, what's the plan?"

"So if you can distract those guards, I think I can tunnel us in."

Charlie started thinking. How to distract all four of them? Archeopteryx were intelligent and too smart to move as one and if he only took out two or even three of them, the plan would still be doomed.

"I've got this," Meredith said.

"Really? What's your plan?" Charlie asked.

"I don't want to overthink it. Just stand over there," Meredith pushed Charlie and the oryctodromeus up against the base of the structure. Then she turned and ran out to a patch of bare, open ground and looked up at the top of the tower.

"Hey," she shouted. She waved her short arms. One of the guards ignored her completely, tucked his beak under one wing and closed his eyes. Only one inched forward on his ledge and peered down at her. "Yeah, you up there. I want in the castle so pick me up. I'm going to give Occidor a piece of my mind."

The guard who had stepped forward took one more step – not jumping from the ledge so much as falling. He leaned forward and dove, beak down. Like an arrow fired from above, wings tucked, spine straight, the archeopteryx kept gaining speed. Meredith fidgeted in place as a faint whistling began to come off of the guard hurtling toward her.

"Does she know what she's doing?" The oryctodromeus asked Charlie.

"Yes," Charlie replied trying to convince himself. "I don't

107

know what she's doing. But she always does."

The archeopteryx showed no signs of stopping or even slowing. Twenty feet away and Charlie knew something was wrong; the guard was going to impale Meredith on its needle-sharp beak. Charlie tried to run to her but the oryctodromeus grabbed his tail – a way that Charlie was unaccustomed to being grabbed – and he fell face-first in the dust.

Just then the archeopteryx's wings burst open. Slowing barely at all, it rotated in mid-air, its gleaming talons now aimed at Meredith. The impact of its snatching strike might break her back. As this was happening though, an orb the size of a soccer ball had formed at Meredith's feet. It swelled faster than any Charlie had ever seen, too fast for the archeopteryx to avoid.

The guard's talons had opened, reaching out for Meredith's flesh at the same moment that she disappeared within a glowing blue dome. The archeopteryx bounced like a rubber ball dropped from the second-floor bannister onto the linoleum of the foyer. The sound was like bagpipes fed into a trash compactor.

"That was awesome," the young oryctodromeus said.

The archeopteryx landed 30 feet away in a heap and didn't move. Now all of the guards were paying attention to Meredith and they were angry.

Two more guards dropped from the tower ledge. About halfway down the tower, they split, looking to flank and pin Meredith between them. Meredith started to run. She turned and ran away from the castle as the two guards determined not to fall into the same trap that the first had, opened their wings, slowed and pursued Meredith from just above the ground. Meredith scrambled over the thin rocky soil and the archeopteryx guards chased after, their beating wings throwing up huge clouds of dust.

One of the guards pulled ahead as she approached the edge of the circle of bare ground and hovered just over Meredith's tail which was whipping fiercely from side to side to keep him back. Meredith dove, disappearing into the tall grass. The guard's talons snapped shut grabbing only wads of grass and it banked sharply upward preparing for another run.

Meanwhile, the trailing guard landed in the grass and began to walk swinging his beak like a scythe searching for Meredith's hiding place.

Charlie had climbed to his feet. He took the young oryctodromeus by the shoulders. "Can you get started? I don't know how much longer she can hide from them."

"Not with him still watching," the dinosaur pointed up to the last guard peering down at them, "As soon as I start digging, he'll come down on us like a bolt of...a bolt of...well, we call it 'lightning.' I don't know what your people -"

"We call it 'lightning' too! I got it."

Back in the field of grass, the guard marched forward slashing the grass with his beak while the archeopteryx in the air circled overhead watching for signs of movement. The walking guard stopped suddenly. He had noticed something, a small rustling. He jogged closer and Meredith stood up – not Meredith the oryctodromeus but Meredith the little girl. The guard staggered backward.

"Can I help you?" Meredith asked.

"Did – did you see an oryctodromeus around here?"

"Hmm...let me think...plates on its back, spiky tail?"

"No, that's a stegosaurus."

"Ok, three horns, head frill?" Meredith was walking closer as they spoke.

"That's a triceratops! I'm looking for an oryctodromeus."

"Oh, oryctoDROmeus. Why didn't you say so? I saw one of those. Let me just tell you where I saw it." Meredith stood right next to the archeopteryx now. She leaned in close and whispered something to him. When she finished, the archeopteryx launched himself off the ground furiously flapping his wings. He turned and flew back toward the castle picking up speed until he collided with the black rock like a bird flying into a clear window. The archeopteryx crumpled and fluttered to the ground.

Meredith stood admiring her work when talons clamped around her shoulders and she was lifted off the ground. The guard who had been circling overhead swooped down and grabbed her from behind. The archeopteryx beat its wings and began to climb. It tipped its head back and let out a triumphant screech.

"What do we do now?" The young oryctodromeus asked Charlie.

"Let me think." Could he throw something – a rock or a tree – at the guard? Meredith would fall 10 stories and it would still leave the guard at the top.

The archeopteryx carrying Meredith continued to climb, somehow it seemed to rise just as quickly as it had fallen and now Charlie couldn't hope to reach it with a projectile. It reached the top of the tower and paused. It hovered in the air and the last guard hopped forward on his perch to get a better look at this creature that had incapacitated two guards.

Meredith squirmed in fear gripping the archeopteryx's talons and wanting him both to set her free and to not let her go. The head guard jerked his beak toward the hole indicating what should be done with the girl.

The flying archeopteryx started to rise again preparing to

release Meredith down the tower shaft and then something odd happened – a flash of light and a popping sound. Charlie was forced to shield his eyes from the glare and when he looked back, three figures were falling from the tower, all of them dazed, lifeless. The two guards' wings hung at their sides flapping in the wind like tattered flags. Meredith fell too, headfirst and limp.

"What happened?" The oryctodromeus asked. But Charlie ignored him. He was searching for something, anything to break Meredith's fall. Everything around them was black rock and dirt.

Meredith's eyes started to flutter.

Charlie yanked the book from his sister's backpack desperate for a spell that would turn soil into water or reverse gravity.

Meredith now halfway down the tower opened her eyes in alarm and realized that the ground was rushing at her very quickly.

Charlie tried to concentrate on the book but he kept stealing looks at Meredith's descent. Seconds remained before she hit the ground.

Meredith, still groggy, glanced to each side and saw the guards falling next to her and with a few quick hand movements she transformed herself into an archeopteryx. Her wings spread; she wobbled and flapped awkwardly like a cat trying to swim. She hit the ground, tumbled in a heap and rolled to a stop. She had slowed her fall just enough to make the landing painful but avoid serious injury. The two guards had not been so lucky.

Charlie ran to the spot where Meredith had landed and found her returned to her human form. Her knees and elbows were scraped raw. She sat in the dirt massaging her temples trying to rub away a tremendous headache.

"What was that?" Charlie asked. "At the top of the tower?"

"It was something I picked up from the book," Meredith said wearily. "Mostly just sound and light. Only really effective at close range. Except I forgot to close my eyes. Stunned myself accidentally."

"So you meant to do that? To get caught? And the last guard? The tower?"

"Yeah, basically. Except the falling part, like I said."

Charlie didn't know what else to say so he simply helped her up and provided a shoulder to lean on as she walked.

"Well...good distraction. I guess we should see how he's doing with the digging."

They returned to the spot where Charlie had left the young oryctodromeus but he was nowhere to be seen. Instead they found a mound of loose dirt and a hole in the ground.

Charlie leaned down, cupped his hand to his mouth and shouted: "Hey, how's it going in there?" He'd barely spoken the last word of his question before the oryctodromeus' head popped up out of the hole, smiling and squinting up at Charlie and Meredith.

"Finished."

CHAPTER TWENTY-FIVE

The oryctodromeus led the way through what must have been nearly a half mile of tunnels. Charlie and Meredith saw numerous side tunnels and branching pathways and were glad the oryctodromeus had chosen to stay with them long enough to guide them through the tunnels.

"Wouldn't a straight line have been easier?" Charlie finally had to ask.

"Well, yes, but I did some asking around in different wings of the prison and I think I can take you right where you need to go. You're looking for the dinosorcerers, right? So that's where we're going."

Meredith and Charlie stayed behind the young oryctodromeus as he followed a map in his head of the underground maze he'd constructed. Meredith remained in her human form. Transforming three times in just a few minutes during her escape from the guards had taken a lot out of her and she didn't think she could attempt it again so soon.

At last, the oryctodromeus stopped at a path that sloped

gently upward. "That's it. You should just have to punch through a foot or so of dirt at the top. Didn't want to leave an open hole in case a guard came by."

Meredith stepped forward and took the oryctodromeus' hand. "Thank you...I'm sorry, we didn't ask your name."

"It's Quintus," he replied. "My parents said they named me after a great dinosorcerer. Do you know him?"

"In a way," Charlie said. "And I know that he would be very proud of you."

Charlie climbed up and began to dig carefully through the layer of soil at the top of the hole. When he broke through and a shaft of light shone down into the tunnel, Charlie put his eye to the opening and peeked through.

"Looks like the coast is clear. Let's go."

He widened the opening and climbed through helping Meredith up after him. They found themselves in the center of a round room. There were a pair of iron doors set on opposite sides of the room. The walls in a full circle around the room were made up of bars, bars that guarded prison cells cut into the rough rock face.

The walls tapered as they rose so the room funneled upward toward a small circle of light. Charlie was staring upward in wonder at the room's conical design when he tripped. Any hope of making a stealthy entrance and exit vanished as the sounds of clanging metal and Charlie's body slamming down on the hard-packed dirt floor echoed around the room.

Charlie looked down at what had tripped him and saw thick, rusty chains attached at one end to blocks of black rock set into the floor and at the other end to a set of shackles.

The prisoners had stepped forward to the bars of their

cells to see where the noise had come from. Their sunken saurian faces materialized from the darkness within their cells and poked through the bars into the dim light from above.

"Meredith, is that you?" Charlie recognized the voice instantly. He and Meredith ran to the cell from which it had come. "What are you doing here?" Beeon asked; then in a weary voice, "and is that?" He inspected the oryctodromeus standing next to her. "Charlie?"

"We're here to help you – all of you – get out," Charlie said. "And then we can stop Occidor together."

The other dinosaurs in the cell groaned and moved away from the bars receding back into the shadows. "Charlie, it's not that simple. I'm afraid you shouldn't have come."

Suddenly the room filled again with the sound of rattling chains. Beeon's eyes jerked upward. "Oh, no. You must hide." A shadow moved through the circle of light above them. It was growing larger, descending toward them.

"Quick, get in here," one of the dinosaurs hissed from the back of the cell. The bars were built to contain adult dinosorcerers so Meredith slipped through easily. Charlie fitted his head and shoulders through without trouble but his wide, lizard hips would not go.

Just then the iron doors were flung open and a pair of pachycephalosaurs entered from either side of the room. They hadn't yet noticed Charlie's back half stuck outside the cell.

"Grab his hands and pull," Beeon whisper-shouted. And Charlie felt hands grab his from out of the shadows and pull. There was an extraordinary painful pressure on his shoulders as well as his hips then a pop and Charlie landed inside the cell.

Charlie looked out at the guards marching closer to the

cell and noticed something there on the ground, something pink with pictures of bunnies and lollipops on it. One of the guards noticed too. He approached it cautiously and lifted it with the spear he was holding.

"Carnix! Stop wasting time. Get one of them into position. Now!" A platform suspended by chains lowered Occidor from the ceiling.

The incident at Beeon's cave had clearly taken its toll on him. He knelt on the platform too weak to stand. Several deep cuts ran along his pebbled hide and he looked somehow smaller. His arms were thinner, more ropey, no longer rippling with muscle.

The guard slung Charlie's sister's backpack over his shoulder and unlocked the cell door. Two of the dinosorcerers pushed Meredith, the human girl, behind them shielding her from the guard's view.

"You," the guard barked, pointing to a stooped old spinosaurus. "Get out here."

The spinosaurus shuffled forward out of the cell. When he reached the center of the room, the two guards forced him to the ground and locked his hands and feet into the shackles Charlie had stumbled over earlier.

"What's he doing?" Charlie whispered to Beeon. But he didn't answer. He turned his face to the ground and closed his eyes very tight.

A red glow washed over the room. It formed in the space in between Occidor's platform and the chained spinosaurus. It grew more solid until a thick column of light rose from the spinosaur's chest. It pulsed like a heartbeat and Occidor slowly rose to his feet. The cuts along his back and shoulders sealed themselves. Then just as quickly as it had started, the beam vanished. The guards rushed in to check on the

116

spinosaurus. One of them looked up nervously to Occidor.

"Well?" Occidor boomed.

"That's all he's got, sir," the guard whined.

"Get him out of there," Occidor bellowed. The guards unchained the spinosaurus and lifted him to his feet. The spinosaurus hung limp between them, his head lolling from side to side as they marched him back to his cell.

"Get me another one," Occidor shouted. "In fact," and a wicked smile crossed his face. "Get me, Beeon. All of this is his fault."

CHAPTER TWENTY-SIX

The guards tossed the spinosaurus back into the cell and grabbed Beeon. He stumbled forward, tried to walk, but his feet scraped the ground as they dragged him toward the shackles.

"Stop!" Charlie yelled. "Take me instead."

"Who is this?" Occidor called down from his platform in irritation.

One of the guards scurried back to the cell and pulled Charlie out. He quickly looked Charlie up and down. "I don't know, sir. Never seen him before," the guard said. "But he looks like he's got plenty in him. Should I hook him up?"

"How long have you worked here?" Occidor asked.

"Two hundred and eighty years, sir. Never missed a day."

"Do you find it strange that, today, there is a new prisoner in our secure prison facility that you've never seen before?"

The guard thought for a moment. "Now that you mention it, it does seem odd, sir."

"We've met before, Occidor," Charlie said. "But you

might recognize me better like this."

Charlie returned to his human form. The guards staggered back in shock.

"Ah, yes. Charlie. I had an annoying feeling I wasn't done with you," Occidor said.

"There are actually two of them," Occidor instructed his guards, "so if you wouldn't mind, please check all the cells to make sure there are no additional surprises." But it wasn't necessary for them to check all of the cells. In the first one they checked, the one that Charlie had come from, they discovered another human, this one a girl.

After the guards had dragged Meredith from the cell and stood her next to Charlie and Beeon in the middle of the room, Occidor spoke: "That should be everyone. Guards, take them to the lower dungeon to await execution."

"Wait," Charlie said. "You don't have to do that. I'm done fighting. I've got what you're looking for. Right here actually." He cautiously approached the guard wearing his sister's backpack.

"Charlie," Meredith whispered.

"What are you doing?" Beeon finished her thought.

Charlie held his hands up to show the guard he meant no harm then reached over his shoulder into the backpack and withdrew the book.

"You're right, Occidor. You deserve this as much as anyone," Charlie said. "I'd like to give it to you."

Charlie held the book out to Occidor.

"Charlie, you can't," Meredith cried.

Occidor leapt from his platform to the ground below. He inspected the book for a moment as if expecting a trick of some kind then slowly, tentatively he grasped the book and plucked it from Charlie's hands. A smile crept across his face and his teeth glinted in the dim light.

"Thank you," Occidor said. "And now, guards, you can take them to the lower dungeon to await execution."

The guards gripped their prisoners by the arms and began to lead them away. "Wait," Charlie called.

"What now?" Occidor growled.

"That makes three," Charlie said.

Occidor looked puzzled.

"Three times I've helped you," Charlie continued. "Let's see, there was the time I conjured you in the cave and revealed to you where Beeon was living. Then I sent that map with Beeon that helped you get back to earth. And now I gave you the book. Three times."

"Yes," Occidor seethed. "That does make three and it would appear that I am in your debt. So...what would you like?"

Charlie was silent. He looked to Beeon hoping he might find some strength or wisdom or bravery there. The ancient dinosaur only gave him a gentle smile in return.

"Well?" Occidor bellowed.

"I – I want you to let us go," Charlie said.

"No, I'm afraid not. I won't do that. I've spent millions of years searching for Beeon. I won't just-"

"Not Beeon," Charlie interrupted. "Us," he pulled Meredith closer. "Just us."

Charlie couldn't look at Beeon now. "We shouldn't have come here. I see that now. Let us go back to earth and we won't bother you again. You stay on this planet; we'll stay on ours."

Occidor let out a hollow chuckle. "That's some bargain. You've taught them to recognize a lost cause at least, Beeon. In keeping with dinosaur tradition, I accept. Guards, take

Beeon back to his cell. And you two, I trust you can show yourselves out?"

Charlie conjured a portal as the guards came to collect Beeon.

Meredith bolted in front of the lumbering pachycephalosaurs and threw her arms around Beeon. "Oh, Beeon, I'm so sorry," she said, her head pressed against his chest.

"Charlie made the right choice. This is how it must be," Beeon told her. "Now, you should go."

Meredith turned and glared at Charlie. He opened his mouth to say something but she stomped past him and disappeared into the portal.

The guards were dragging Beeon away. "I didn't know what else to do," Charlie shouted across the room to him.

"You did your best," Beeon said calmly, "and that means a great deal."

Charlie couldn't watch anymore, the way the guards roughly tossed Beeon into his cramped dark cell and slammed shut the cell door.

Charlie turned to face the portal ready to leave all of this behind. But as he took a step towards it, the portal folded itself and, with a soft 'pop,' it vanished.

"Oops," Occidor said. "Those portals can be so difficult to hold open, particularly for an untrained beast like yourself."

"I didn't do that," Charlie objected.

"No. I did," Occidor barked. "Did you think I could trust you to leave and never interfere in my affairs again, never try to rescue Beeon? Oh, come on, I'm not that foolish. No, in a day or a week you would be right back here where you are now, at my mercy. I'm just saving us all some time."

"The girl could go. I never saw any talent in her. But you've got something special, something that, with the right teacher, could be developed into greatness or could be...snuffed out. Which would you like, Charlie?"

Charlie stood speechless. What exactly was Occidor proposing?

"You could be very helpful in reclaiming the earth," Occidor said. "Act as my ambassador, my spokesman. Tell your people they have nothing to fear from becoming my servants. Join me and you might have a kingdom of your own someday."

Occidor attempted a warm smile but his face seemed to struggle against it. Charlie watched this battle between lips and teeth for an uncomfortably long time before he spoke.

"To tell you the truth, I don't do well with teachers – just ask Mrs. Bookman at Parkville Elementary. Luckily I have friends to help me through. The kind of friends who can memorize every constellation visible in the northern hemisphere and will miss going out to the movies with her family to help you practice them or the kind who can learn a spell just by seeing it performed once."

"It's true the spells come naturally to me but I always seem to make a critical mistake. Like when I conjured you instead of any other dinosaur on this planet. Or when I missed earth by 72 light years and instead opened a portal 15 feet away." Occidor wheeled around searching the room. "Straight up."

Occidor jerked his head upward and saw Meredith's face beaming down from his platform. He tried to run but the column of light caught and held him fast. His muscles deflated like ruptured pool toys.

He howled not in pain but frustration and then he began

to shrink. First to the size of a common corythosaurus, then an oryctodromeus, then a compsognathus and finally the size of an iguana.

He gripped the book to his chest as long as he could until his hands became too small to hold it. The book tumbled to the ground landing first on its side then falling flat just an inch away from squashing the lizard-sized Occidor. He scurried off in fear, disappearing down the hole in the floor where Charlie and Meredith had entered.

The guards seemed to consider staying and fighting for a moment until they looked up and saw Meredith standing 20 feet tall on the platform above them.

"Don't try me," Meredith's voice rattled the walls.

The guards dropped their spears and Charlie's sister's backpack and ran for the iron doors.

CHAPTER TWENTY-SEVEN

The job of setting free the dinosorcerers fell to Charlie because Meredith was finding it difficult to navigate the room at her current height.

More than once Charlie was nearly trampled by the T-Rex-sized Meredith.

After Charlie had opened all of the cells, Meredith returned to her spot on the platform and worked the spell in reverse. The dinosorcerers formed a line and took turns standing under the beam Meredith projected.

Dinosaurs stepped into the light looking malnourished and ancient and emerged renewed. They stood tall again. Their eyes were bright and quick.

Meredith kept going until the last dinosaur in line, Beeon, had been revived and until she had run off all – or nearly all – of the energy she'd absorbed from Occidor.

She climbed down from the platform and stood next to Charlie. He squinted and inspected her closely. "Didn't you used to be shorter than me?"

Meredith shrugged. "Growth spurt."

Beeon smiled at them both. He had a vitality Charlie hadn't seen in him before. He was reunited with his friends and they were free now to begin building the world Quintus had envisioned for them, a world of enlightenment and magic working together to benefit all dinosaurs.

"Occidor was very wrong about you, Meredith," Beeon said. "You are one of the finest sorcerers I have ever met. But he was right about you, Charlie. You have a natural talent." He cleared his throat and went on. "I imagine you two need to be getting back to your parents. But...you know the way to this planet now and...."

Charlie thought at first that Beeon had lost his train of thought but, no, he realized that Beeon was struggling with a question he'd waited 65 million years to ask.

A sly smirk spread across Charlie's face. "Beeon, are you asking us...."

"Will you be my apprentices?" Beeon blurted out.

The same smirk affixed itself to Meredith's face. "I don't know...what do you think, Charlie? Should we talk this over?" Beeon sighed deeply.

"I think I speak for both of us," Charlie said, "when I say, 'are you out of your mind? Yes!'"

"Oh, good," Beeon let out a relieved chuckle. "Tuesdays and Thursdays, 4:30, work for you?"

"Sure," Charlie said. "But there's more. An oryctodromeus named Quintus – good digger – should be waiting outside the castle for you. And he might have friends."

"I'll make sure there are plenty of seats," Beeon said.

Charlie picked up his sister's backpack and created another portal, to earth this time, just past the soccer fields.

The single sun would be going down when they returned.

They'd walk home past children riding bikes, climbing trees.

They would make it home just in time for dinner, brush their teeth, climb into bed, and in the morning, Charlie and Meredith would begin counting down the seconds until Tuesday.

THE END

Thank you for reading. If you enjoyed the book, please consider leaving a review. Reviews and recommendations are crucial to independent publishers.

Cover design by Nathan Milner with assets from Vecteezy.com and from zoey at pngtree.com.

Made in the USA
Middletown, DE
10 April 2020